Beasts
of England

Beasts of England

ADAM BILES

GALLEY BEGGAR PRESS

First published in 2023
By Galley Beggar Press Limited
37 Dover Street, Norwich, NR2 3LG

A CIP for this book is available from the British Library

Paperback ISBN: 978-1-913111-45-8
Black cover edition ISBN: 978-1-913111-46-5

Text and design by Tetragon, London
Printed and bound in Great Britain by CPI Books, Chatham

For A. & A.

WILLINGDON COURIER

MANOR CHOOZES BUTTERCUP... AGAIN!

Syme, Manor Farm, Wealden

IN A RESULT THAT ruffled precisely no feathers, Buttercup the pig – leader of the Manor Farm Animalists – yesterday secured a sixth victory in the Wealden estate's annual 'Choozin'. The victory makes Buttercup the second longest serving First Beast in Manor Farm's history, behind only Traviata the formidable sow – of the opposing 'Jonesists' – who served for seven and a half terms, more than a decade ago.

A victory for Buttercup always seemed assured, and as the walnuts were counted the returning First Beast couldn't suppress a smile that made him look as happy as a pig in muck. Not that there's much muck on Manor Farm these days. The estate has never looked better than under Buttercup's stewardship. Outbuildings have been replaced, paths have been gravelled. Coop, stable and vivarium alike have been fitted with every mod-con… all paid for by the money generated by the farm's famous windmill and its miraculously efficient turbine.

A HARD ROW TO HOE

It's a remarkable transformation for a farm that was long considered 'Wealden's Runt'. The first estate in England to shake off human rule, Animal Farm – as it was briefly known – rapidly fell under the despotic rule of Napoleon, a devious porker who abused the greenness of his liberated comrades while betraying the beliefs that had fuelled the original rebellion

('ALL ANIMALS ARE EQUAL'). Exhaustion, despair and destitution followed.

After Napoleon was shipped off to the great knacker in the sky, Manor Farm lived through many shaky years before a 'Council of Animals' was established and the first 'Choozin' held. It then took almost another decade for Manor Farm's proud and suspicious beasts to take their rightful place at the heart of the Wealden Union of Farmers (WUF), founded – as many readers will know – to allow our Sussex smallholdings to compete against the industrial farms of Hampshire, Surrey, and Kent. Although even then it was said that Manor Farm only joined because Traviata wanted to expand the market for the windmill's electricity, and so fund the controversial transformation

of the holding from a traditional working estate to the profitable petting farm it is today.

SUNLIT PLOUGHLANDS

But all of this turbulent history felt like a distant memory last night as Buttercup took a victory lap of the farmyard on his hind trotters. Neither a recent kerfuffle over the sumptuous redecoration of the farmhouse, nor his ongoing, costly support of the Shore Farm rebellion, has dented his popularity.

AUGUST

I t was a Sunday in late summer. The last of the visitors had left, the floor of the cowshed had been scrubbed, the chicks had been counted and locked in their coop, and the lights in the vivarium had been turned off. Another long week on Manor Farm was over. On any other evening the animals would have taken to their beds as soon as their chores were finished. But this was not any other evening. This evening, there was a fluttering and stirring across the farm as beast and fowl alike converged on the Big Barn. First came the sheep and alpacas, who jostled for the best spot at the beer troughs, while the rabbits bobbed between their hooves hoping to catch any splashed dregs. Then came the cows, among them Clive the Bullock and Marguerite the aged Holstein, who was looking for a bed of straw to settle upon after her long walk up from the large pasture. A dozen hens roosted in the eaves by the door, the pigeons lined up along the edge of the cash desk, and the geckos congregated on the vast east window. Cassie the mule came in, moving carefully so as not to step on a gang of rats. She was closely followed by Flaxen, the roe deer, and a gaggle of geese. One of the geese, Haw-Haw, was already deep in conversation with the farm's stocky bull terriers, Dunning and Kruger, whose gold teeth flashed as they quit the dusk of the farmyard for the well-lit barn. A trio of magpies had perched, with characteristic aloofness, atop the postcard carousel, and a family of dormice had settled in the display of plush toys. The animals kept coming, score upon score, until every patch of floor, every inch of rafter, every tabletop, and every book display, was occupied by trotter, hoof, talon, paw and foot. Finally, the pigs swaggered in on their hind trotters, acting like they owned the place. And tonight, in a sense, one of them did.

His name was Buttercup, and he had just begun his sixth term as Manor Farm's First Beast. He was a lean boar, with a firm gut, a charming grin and a youthful air, although the strain of running the farm for over five years had carved deep creases around his eyes. Buttercup was a canny steward who'd spent freely from Manor Farm's coffers to bolster his popularity among every species. The past season alone his Council of Animals had voted to repaint the grain store, fix the thermostat of the vivarium, and hire a dray of squirrels from a nearby wood to collect visitors' litter and remove it to the quarry, a task formerly shared between the farm's sheep and alpacas.

And how was all this spending possible? Thanks, in large part, to the money that Dunning and Kruger made selling the windmill's electricity to neighbouring farms and beyond. The First Beast knew that few on the farm understood how the windmill made so much money. And, in truth, he didn't really understand it himself. But he also knew that as long as they had sufficient food in their troughs and bodies unbroken by physical toil, most of the animals, pigs included, were happy to leave such details to the dogs.

Buttercup's most impressive feat, however, and the reason for tonight's gathering, was the reconstruction of the Big Barn itself, which had fallen into disrepair and disuse many years earlier. In fact, the new Big Barn was no barn at all, but a brick, glass and steel building housing a purpose-built information centre and gift shop. Since the start of July, visitors to 'the South of England's Premium Petting Zoo' had trooped through the Big Barn's newly opened doors to pick up maps in a variety of languages, swap cash for 'Manor Pounds' and buy detailed scale models of the farm's famous windmill. Although many of the animals resented the uncouth and handsy behaviour of the farm's mostly-human sightseers, they only had to think of the plough-pulling, egg-laying, milk-pumping, meat-providing lives of their ancestors for that resentment to quickly vanish.

Tonight was the Big Barn's official opening, and Buttercup had let it be known that two surprise finishing touches would be unveiled; one on the western wall, and the other on the east window. Both were hidden behind tarpaulins, and had been the subject of much excited speculation among Manor Farm's animals.

On this Sunday evening in late summer, the animals were pleased with Buttercup, and he was very pleased with himself. When he trotted into the Big Barn, accompanied by Cosmo the owl, his dependable Quartermaster, Buttercup was welcomed with the clatter of hooves and trotters, and the beating of wings. Buttercup quieted the gathering with a swipe of his trotter:

'Now's not the time for speeches,' he said. 'And yet, as we stand together beneath the beautiful vaulted roof of *our* new Big Barn, I see not just a building, but a symbol of everything we have achieved. Together. For today, on Manor Farm, rest days are no longer as rare as hens' teeth. Today, on Manor Farm, our mule gives no more than seven rides a day, and never to a human child over ten years old. Today, on Manor Farm, we have abolished undignified costumes for all animals. Today, on Manor Farm, those animals that can work are justly rewarded, and those that cannot are cared for. Today, on Manor Farm, we summoned the compassion and solidarity to help the animals of Shore Farm overthrow the tyrant Percy Cox!' Unsure whether to boo the tyrant or cheer his overthrow, the gathered animals settled for a kind of unruly lowing.

Buttercup might have said this was not the moment for speeches; nevertheless, he continued to deliver a version of the very speech he had given daily in the week preceding the annual Choozin, two months earlier, on the summer solstice. That day,

Buttercup's drove of Animalists had seen off the opposing Jonesist drove for the sixth time in a row, proving – as Buttercup took much relish in declaring almost every time he opened his mouth – that Manor Farm had 'turned definitively away from the old-fashioned, nostalgic, penny-pinching, human-lovers of the Jonesists, and towards the nimble, generous, welcoming, embrace of *Modern Animalism*'.

As Buttercup let the lowing fade, Ribbons, the new leader of the Jonesist pigs, watched from his comfortable armchair in the Big Barn's gallery with a look of grudging admiration. But Ribbons too had his reasons to be smug. In the recent contest to lead his drove, he had bested Curly, a Baston pig with a squashed face and a thick pelt of fur which, from a distance, often saw him mistaken for a sheep. Curly was Ribbons's superior in intelligence and experience, but he was his inferior in looks and charm. For Ribbons was a young, handsome boar, tall when on his hind legs, with a daintily curved snout, a muscular chest and a pinched belly. And though Curly's more traditional Jonesist views (parsimony, deference to humans, and an antagonistic approach to Manor Farm's old enemies, Foxwood and Pinchfield) were more in line with those of the rest of the drove, Ribbons had convinced them that, up against Buttercup, it would take looks and charm to win. And, after six consecutive losses, winning was all that counted.

Buttercup went on:

'Which is why it is an enormous honour for me to be among you this evening to celebrate the reopening of the Big Barn, and to reveal not one, but two monuments which, I believe, go some small way to honouring our collective endeavour.'

Buttercup nodded. The first tarpaulin fell. The animals gasped, cawed and trilled. The bricks of the western wall, bare since the day they had been laid, were now covered, ground to roof, with a splendid mural. The painting was aglow with bright colours and vivid depictions of several dozen episodes from Manor Farm's long history.

'That's Old Major!' bleated one sheep, pointing with a hoof at a stately-looking boar halfway up the painting. 'The leader of the Great Rebellion.'

'Don't you mean Napoleon?' a magpie asked.

'*Who?*' answered the sheep, with a glare.

'Look! That's when the foxes were chased from Manor Farm!' clucked a hen.

'And there's Traviata,' simpered Clive the Bullock, 'selling off the last plough.'

'Is that the Siege of Pinchfield?' a young alpaca asked, indicating a scuffle just above the doorway.

'Imbecilic longneck,' snorted Curly. 'Can't you see that those are *Foxwood* colours?'

'Foxwood. Pinchfield,' said Balmoral the roe deer patriarch. 'Surely, dear Baston, those two putrid farms are much of a muchness anyway?' Curly smiled wryly at this.

In the background stood the familiar silhouette of the old farmhouse, picked out against the bright blue sky of an idyllic summer morning. And above it all, looming over the outbuildings and the animals, its tower soaring so high that it tapered almost to a point near the roof of the barn, was the windmill. A sly optical trick made it seem as if the brilliant white sails were folding the farm and its inhabitants in four caring, maternal arms.

'It's magnificent,' sighed Marguerite the Holstein, her eyes welling with tears.

Buttercup pushed on:

'In short, brothers and sisters,' he patted at his forehead with a handkerchief (a strange affectation since, like all his kind, he had no sweat glands). 'In short, we have truly made sure, for the first time in its history, that our farm lives up to the eternal motto of our heroic founders, that…'

Now he gestured at the east window of the Big Barn. On cue, the second tarpaulin fell. High up on the glass the farm's old motto had been engraved in blocky bevelled letters. Seen from inside the barn the words read back-to-front – but most of the literate animals recognised them at once. Buttercup read them aloud:

('ALL ANIMALS ARE MORE EQUAL THAN OTHERS!')

A rapturous cheer went up. Buttercup nodded to Cosmo the owl, who lowered the needle of an old record player onto a scuffed disc, and the opening bars of Manor Farm's sacred hymn echoed around the Big Barn. Even though few of the animals knew more than the first lines of this song, they broke into it now:

'Beasts of England, Beasts of Ireland,
Beasts of every land and clime,
Dum-de-dum-dum joyful tidings,
Dum-de golden future time!'

Now that Buttercup's speech was over, the Animalist pigs started throwing food at the Jonesists, who fought back with jets of beer spurted straight from the bottle. The sheep and alpacas bleated *'all animals… are more equal… than others'*, and a flock of drunk pigeons sang that one verse of 'Beasts of England' over and over. As for Dunning and Kruger, the bull terriers had climbed to the raised gallery, and were leaning over the railing watching the pandemonium. Their muscles were twitching beneath their fine, bristly pelts, and they were smoking chubby cigars, which twisted their serrated lips into what looked – from below at least – like snarls of immense satisfaction.

Martha, the Brent goose, hopped onto one of the display tables (plastic key-rings, giant pencils…) to get a better look at the new mural. She was the youngest of the gaggle of domesticated geese, whose role on the farm had long been to tell the other animals just what the pigs were getting up to – and so, the hope went, restrain their more human instincts. She was the only Brent goose on a farm of greylags, having hatched from a solitary egg found buried in the reeds around the drinking pool. An egg most likely abandoned or forgotten by one of the wild geese who sometimes stopped over on Manor Farm during their migrations. Martha's outsider status only made her more determined to be of use. The gaggle's work was noble, Martha felt, and she believed in it – despite the fact she spent most of her time doing odd jobs for the other geese and sitting in on boring and mostly puzzling sessions of the Council of Animals.

One way in which she might be useful, she thought, was in making head and tail of the new mural for any animal who had neither the time nor the learning to do so for themselves. Martha prided herself on having memorised how many years after the Great Rebellion each of the important events in the farm's history had taken place. This was something most of the animals seemed to take little interest in, although perhaps that had to do with the vastly different lifespans of the farm's various species.

Looking at the mural with these dates in mind, it suddenly felt more like a pictorial maze, thought up to befuddle any animal who dared set foot in it, than a straightforward telling of Manor Farm's history. There were beautiful depictions of eggs, milk and wool. These were the three famous pillars of Manor Farm's early fortunes but had not been sold for many a year. And while the

Great Rebellion against the humans led by Old Major the boar (Was that even *right*? Could it have been Old Captain? And was he even a boar?) took pride of place alongside depictions of the founding of the Council of Animals (fifteen years after the Great Rebellion), and the Choozins that selected them, there was no hint of the five brutal and turbulent years the farm had endured between these two events. Then, of course, Traviata, the formidable old Jonesist sow – with her inimitable quiffed hairpiece and pearl necklace – was celebrated in the mural for installing the new dynamo room beneath the windmill (22GR?), and for overseeing the farm's transformation from a flagging working estate to a popular petting zoo (26GR… or was it 27?). But where was the turmoil Traviata had inspired by allowing the dogs and pigs to enrich themselves as the rest of the farm fell into ruin? This unrest had been so serious that even all these years later the pigeons and rats still sang songs about it, while the very mention of Traviata's name raised cries of detestation from the ploughland to the spinney. Quarrels with other estates, those that Manor Farm won, at least, took up a lot of the wall, whereas its recent peaceful and fruitful membership of the Wealden Union of Farms (25GR–present day), in brotherhood with many of the very same farms, wasn't pictured anywhere. Although that may be because a scuffle just makes for better eye-fodder than a trotter on a treaty, Martha thought. A painting of a battle is more satisfying to the eye than the depiction of the painstaking removal of barbed wire from the farm's boundaries. A revolutionary stampede is more exciting than the representation of the convoluted negotiations to bring an end to the ancient animosity that had existed when all farms in the county were run by human drunkards, who had frequently sought to undercut and bankrupt each other.

Martha was so engrossed that she didn't notice Cassie standing alongside her until the young mule spoke:

'Who decided which animals to include, do you think?'

'The Council of Animals, I imagine,' Martha said, suddenly finding an answer, or part of one, to her riddle. 'I'm sure the design was negotiated between the Animalists and Jonesists. A prime spot for Old Major, but only if Traviata is celebrated. That kind of thing. Otherwise, after each Choozin it would just get painted over with a new line-up.' Martha hopped onto a low stool so that she and Cassie were on the same eye level. What a curious creature she was up close, with her long ears, pendulous head and intelligent eyes, filled with that last-of-her-line melancholia, the fate of all her kind.

'It's just there's someone I would have expected…' Cassie swallowed, bared her teeth. 'Someone I would have *hoped* to see here, that's all.'

Martha looked back at the mural. There were plenty of episodes she would have expected to see, but she couldn't think of any particular animal that was missing.

'Do you mind if I ask who?'

A wistful look settled on Cassie's face.

'My father,' she said. 'My mother, Gypsy, told me once that there was no history of Manor Farm without him. That when it was sung or…' She flicked her long nose at the wall. 'Or painted, I suppose, that he'd be among its heroes.'

Martha felt perplexed. She couldn't think of any of the farm's heroes that might fit the bill.

'He vanished before I was born,' Cassie continued. 'My mother only spoke about him when she drank, so the descriptions were always patchy. And nobody else I've spoken to seems to have heard of him at all.'

'What was his name?' Martha asked.

Cassie hung her long head.

'I don't know,' she said, sadly.

'Still, perhaps if you could convince the Council of his impor-
tance to our story,' Martha said, 'he might be added to the mural.'
She didn't really believe this, but just then it felt important to
her whole idea of Manor Farm that it might, at the very least,
be possible. Cassie looked pensive.

'How would I do that?'

Martha hesitated. What she was about to say felt indiscreet,
like lifting the curtain on the secrets of the gaggle. But as a
foundling who had never known her parents and never would,
she couldn't bring herself to condemn another animal to the same
fate, if there was any way she could help.

'When us geese can't find what we're looking for, we visit the
old quarry.'

Manor Farm had been dumping its refuse in the quarry for
generations, ever since the supply of stone – the very stone that
built the windmill – had depleted. A rocky patch, half an acre
in size, on the road between Manor Farm and Pinchfield, it had
slowly filled with discarded building materials, fodder barrels and
rusting machine parts – but also newspapers, magazines, receipts
and records which the Council no longer needed, or for which
there was no longer space in the farmhouse cellar. The quarry
was legendary among the geese as a trove of information that
successive generations of pigs had decided was best forgotten. In
truth, it had been a long time since any of the gaggle had spent
much time there. Martha, as a young recruit, had only ever heard
it spoken of, and was yet to make her first visit.

Still, the idea seemed to please Cassie. She was about to thank
Martha when a terrible screech filled the air.

It was one of the hens, who had left the festivities to check up on her chicks. She shrieked again. All the animals in the Big Barn looked first at the door, then at Buttercup.

After a moment's hesitation, the First Beast nodded. He squared his shoulders, set his jaw into a determined jut, and marched across the tiled floor and out of the door. Reassured by Buttercup's resolve, several of the other animals followed. The sight that awaited them was quite unlike anything they had imagined. The hen hadn't been warning of a break-in by stray animals. Nor were towering storm clouds rolling in from the horizon to devastate Manor Farm's apple and pear crops. Nor was one or other of the outbuildings aflame. What the animals saw as they left the Big Barn was Buttercup standing stock still in the farmyard, his immaculate snout pointing upwards, his dark, round eyes fixed on the sky above, watching hundreds and hundreds of starlings twisting and gyrating, forming vast abstract shapes against the purple twilit sky. Whistler, the scrawniest of all the tame magpies, who'd got his name on account of the high-pitched timbre of his caw, hopped up onto on a post beside Buttercup.

'What is it?' asked Buttercup.

'I don't know,' Whistler wheezed. He looked down at his own clipped wings for a moment then up again at the sky. 'But it's beautiful.' And it was. Like a weightless, pulsating blob of television static.

Suddenly, a flank of a hundred or so birds broke off from the main flock, performed a dizzying loop-the-loop, and plunged towards the farmyard, corkscrewing straight into the prize hydrangea bush with the ferocity of a raiding party. The birds tore through the plant with such speed that all that was left once they'd departed was a stripped, twiggy skeleton, and several hundred brightly coloured petals drifting slowly to the ground.

More of the animals had left the Big Barn now, and all were looking to Buttercup for an explanation of what they had just seen. The First Beast snorted several times under his breath.

'I won't lie to you, and claim I know where these birds have come from,' he told the gathering in a very deliberate and measured tone. 'But I will do everything in my power to make sure they leave as quickly as they arrived.'

It soon became clear that, contrary to Buttercup's assurances, the starlings had no plans to leave and he could do nothing to make them. Morning and night, when the animals rose, and when they retired, they were there; perched on the rooftops, and chimney stacks, and fences and gateposts, rattling and chirruping, sometimes in large groups, sometimes alone. Most of the time they warbled away in a language that none of the animals could understand, but every so often, a recognisable but seemingly random word would be picked up by an alpaca making his way across the farmyard, or a hen basking in the sun on top of the coop. Several times during the day, packs of the starlings took wing and performed the most spectacular aerial dances, designing extraordinary silhouettes in the heavens for several minutes, apparently quite indifferent to the activity on the farm below.

One evening, about a week after the birds arrived, Martha the goose had sat through a particularly excitable Council meeting. The pigs had spent several hours arguing over the price of fodder, when Curly the Jonesist had risen to his hind trotters and grunted that the controls imposed on fodder by the WUF were designed 'purely for the enrichment of Foxwood and Pinchfield. Animals across the rest of England eat better than Manor Farm beasts… and cheaper too,' he said, before being shouted down by Animalist and Jonesist alike, for peddling, as Ribbons said, 'cock-and-bull of the very first order'. After which Ribbons was censured by Buttercup for his offensive and outdated turn of phrase.

As Martha the goose made her way across the deserted farmyard, she noticed Whistler standing quite still on a fence post. Since the flock had arrived, he'd not returned to the plush confines of the harness room where the other magpies studied.

Instead he'd spent his days hopping from one corner of the farmyard to another, observing the starlings from every vantage point his clipped wings allowed, eavesdropping on their chattering and, when they took flight, scrutinising their gyrations with an increasingly obsessive gaze.

Martha watched Whistler watching the starlings, almost as intrigued by him as he was by the other birds. Martha had never spoken to Whistler before, and was intimidated by the magpies' reputation for uncommon intelligence. But after several minutes she summoned up her courage.

'Which bird is in charge?' she asked. Whistler started. He'd been so fixated on the starlings that he hadn't noticed Martha's approach.

'None of them,' Whistler said. 'As far as I can tell.'

'And yet their wonderful dances,' said Martha. 'Surely they can't be an accident?' Whistler didn't reply. Not because he had nothing to say on the matter, Martha felt, but because he didn't want to share whatever he knew with her.

'Where did they come from?' Martha tried again. This time Whistler answered.

'It took me a while to understand that,' he said. 'They didn't come from anywhere. They were always here. In the spinney, and the hedgerows, and the eaves of our outbuildings. We just never paid them any mind until now.'

SEPTEMBER

Early autumn was the apple- and pear-picking season. Although the gathering and threshing of the grain crops had long been mechanised, fruit-picking still required bestial labour. In recent years several families of itinerant squirrels had been invited onto the farm for the duration of the harvest, because all of the farm's inhabitants agreed that it was better such labour be undertaken by any beasts but themselves.

So when Buttercup announced to the Council of Animals – gathered in the farmhouse dining room for its weekly session – that Manor Farm could not afford to pay the squirrels this year, the news was greeted by pigs from both droves with confusion and dismay.

'After all the money you spent on ousting Percy Cox on Shore Farm?' sneered Ribbons, snuffling an easy win. Buttercup's snout twitched.

'You can't put a price on justice,' he said. A clicking was heard from one corner of the room. It was Curly. He was playing with a circular slide rule. When he realised he was being watched he pulled a thin smile.

'Tell that to the sheep,' he muttered.

Buttercup pushed on. Several customers, both within the Wealden Union of Farmers and without, had failed to honour their payments for the windmill's electricity, and so Manor Farm's summer takings were marginally lower than forecast. It was nothing to worry about, he assured them. The dogs Dunning and Kruger were already in talks with new customers to make up the shortfall, and any tightening of the bridles was only a temporary measure. The simple fact was, Buttercup insisted, if Manor Farm wanted to profit from the orchard's abundant yield this year, Manor beasts would have to pick and gather the fruit themselves.

Buttercup assigned the task of arranging the harvest to his Quartermaster Cosmo. The dour tawny owl was known to enjoy finding the most rational organisation for more or less any activity. On the day the harvest was due to begin, he called the sheep, geckos and alpacas, as well as Cassie the mule, to the orchard. A moth-eaten bedsheet had been strung between two of the trees, on which were drawn several crude depictions of apple and pear trees, as well as sketches of each of the summoned animals, and a series of confusing arrows. Cosmo was standing on a barrel positioned beside the sheet. In his talons he gripped a telescopic car aerial, flotsam from the visitors' car park no doubt. He extended it with a satisfying metallic ripple.

'The most logical organisation of the harvest,' he began, whacking the sheet with the aerial. 'Will involve the geckos' – *whack!* – 'loosening the higher fruit' – *whack!* – with their teeth, so causing them to fall into hay-lined baskets, which' – *whack!* – 'will be strapped to the backs of the sheep.' Several of the sheep grunted in consternation at this, causing Cosmo to lose his grip on the aerial. It fell to the grass.

'Meanwhile our friends the alpacas, with their stately necks and sturdy legs, will pick fruit from the lower-hanging branches, and collect windfall from the grass. These too will be deposited on the sheep's backs, before being carried to Cassie, who will tip the baskets into the sorting barrels.' Cosmo hopped down from the barrel, collected the aerial, and collapsed it with evident relish. 'Any questions?'

At first, the sheep grumbled. Previous generations of their species had laboured in precisely this way so that they would not have to.

'Do you think we can't see,' one of them bleated, 'that we're the only native species being put to work in this way?' A remark that confused Cassie, and upset the alpacas, many of whom were the fourth generation of their kind to be born on Manor Farm.

'Why don't we just use some of the Pile?' One of the sheep asked. 'If the shortfall is temporary?'

The Pile was what the animals called the several tons of cereal crops stored in the largest silo in the farmyard. It had been filled a decade or so earlier with grain purchased from Foxwood for a good price, and kept in reserve should Manor Farm's own crops fail one year.

'As I'm sure you know,' Cosmo said, a strange quiver to his voice. 'To access the Pile we would have to break the silo's airtight seal. This would significantly shorten the life of any grain we didn't then sell. And besides, by the time we found a buyer, and employed the squirrels, most of the apples and pears would have already ripened, fallen and rotted. No, the Pile is for a rainy day. Today's sky is filled with a few wispy clouds. They'll soon disappear.'

'Then what about the cows?' a second sheep complained. 'Surely they can carry baskets just as well as us?'

'And why were the pigeons and the rats not also put to work?' moaned a third. 'I don't suppose it has anything to do with the pigs being scared of their feral ways?'

Cosmo took the sheep aside and assured them that even though they would have baskets on their backs, in many ways their role was managerial, and they'd be rewarded better than the other animals for their work. Hearing this, the sheep agreed to participate, although without much enthusiasm.

'I understand we're asking a lot of you,' Cosmo concluded. 'But I want you to know that, at one time or another, and in one way or another, every animal will be asked to pitch in.'

And so the sheep, and the geckos, and the alpacas, and Cassie took to the orchard with a sense of relief that at least they would have made their share of sacrifices, and next time it would be the turn of others.

wo large sorting barrels were installed in the farmyard. One had a sign that read APPLES and another a sign that read PEARS. It was around noon that Cosmo noticed the barrel marked APPLES was actually half-full of pears, and the one marked PEARS had only apples in it. Cosmo called Cassie over:

'We all thoroughly appreciate the work you're doing, of course,' he said, pointing out the error. 'But perhaps a little more concentration is called for?'

'Maybe I was a little distracted,' Cassie said to Cosmo, her muzzle dipping with embarrassment. She'd been thinking about Martha the goose again, and her advice to visit the quarry. Indeed, she'd been thinking about the quarry a good deal lately.

Once the mistake had been discovered, and once the sheep had finished grumbling about it, the embarrassed mule began laboriously putting it right, emptying the barrel marked PEARS one apple at a time, being careful not to damage the fruit with her teeth. While the other animals stopped for lunch, Cassie worked, moving apple after apple, until her eyes glazed and her sides grew matted with sweat. When about half the apples were piled in the farmyard, Cosmo came hopping over to Cassie:

'How foolish of me!' he exclaimed. 'How unreasonable!'

'What…' Cassie said, her vast sternum expanding and contracting like a set of bellows. 'Was… unreasonable?'

'My instruction,' Cosmo said. 'Of course it would have been much easier just to swap the signs!' Cassie looked from the barrels to the pile of apples, then to Cosmo, then back to the barrels. Cosmo was smiling with complicity at Cassie, as if the foolishness was theirs to share. 'So if you wouldn't mind just putting those apples back where you found them, while I take care of the signs, that would be tremendous.'

Later that afternoon, however, Cassie noticed that the signs had been switched back. Once again Cosmo rearranged them and once again work resumed, although only for about a quarter of an hour, when it was noticed that the signs had been exchanged a third time, despite Cassie now keeping a scrupulous, if exhausted, watch over the barrels. When it happened a fourth time, and a fifth, and still no culprit had been identified, Cosmo decided that it had become so tiresome keeping track of the signs that another solution was needed. He called a break and gathered the fruit-picking animals in the courtyard to explain his idea.

'What if,' he said, 'for the duration of this harvest, we take to calling apples pears, and pears apples? Perhaps, then, our mysterious mischief-maker might allow us to get on with, and even finish, our work.'

The geckos and alpacas agreed. Both species already had alternative words for each fruit, brought by their parents and grandparents from distant climes. Cassie, too, was unconcerned. The difference between apples and pears had never seemed very significant to her anyway. But the sheep objected. They had always called apples 'apples' and pears 'pears' and could not see why they should do otherwise now.

'You know,' Cosmo said, a slightly desperate edge to his voice. 'If I retained one thing from the year I spent studying with the magpies, it's that there's no *real* reason for the word apple to be attributed to the rounder of the two fruits, and the word pear to the more bell-shaped variety. Words, after all, only acquire meaning in the wider context of the language in which they exist.'

When the sheep met this explanation with bleats of equal parts incomprehension and derision, Buttercup, who'd been watching from a distance, stepped forward. He narrowed his eyes and spoke to the sheep like an affronted parent:

'Let me tell you that I consider it a profound shame that you choose to be so stubborn about this. Apple and pear are human words, after all. The renaming of things is not only the right, but the duty of every free animal. Surely you recall the fourth verse of "Beasts of England"?' At which, he cleared his throat and sang:

> *'Cast aside the tyrant's language,*
> *Control of our minds we seize,*
> *Apples, Pears and Mangel–Wurzels,*
> *Ours to name howe'er we please!'*

The sheep exchanged chastened glances, ashamed to have forgotten these lines. While they were not completely at ease with the switching of fruit names, neither did they want to appear as allies of humans and the old ways. And so, with a chorus of baas, they accepted Buttercup's argument and set about committing the unfamiliar verse to memory. Cassie was quite certain those were not the words to "Beasts of England", but hoped that perhaps they could now finish their work, untroubled by the joker in their midst. And so it proved, for once all the animals had accepted the change, the signs remained in place and their work was able to find its original rhythm again.

After the animals had been working for several days, a pigeon landed on the edge of the PᴧRꟼꟄ barrel. It was clear she had something to say:

'It was the starlings!' she cooed.

'What was the starlings?' Cosmo asked.

'Switching the signs!' she said. 'They did it in gangs, whenever the mule was distracted!'

Since no rational explanation could be found for the birds' actions, Cosmo put it down to simple mischief-making, and no more thought was given to it.

As the apple-picking (that's to say pear-picking) season concluded several weeks before the pear-picking (that's to say apple-picking) season, a van arrived to the collect the apples (that's to say pears) and take them off to market before they rotted. Left with only the pears (that's to say apples) now, Cosmo suggested they revert to the former names. He was surprised when the sheep loudly objected to any return to the human words. The alpacas agreed. So much energy had been wasted, and so much confusion caused by the constant name swapping, surely it would be easier to leave things as they were. And not just until the pear-picking (that's to say apple-picking) was done, but afterwards too. As the change seemed to cause no harm, and fighting it would take much more of the tired animals' energy than just agreeing, it was decided that from then on, apples would forever be pears and pears would forever be apples. If, of course, the starlings allowed it to be so.

When the pears (that's to say apples) had also been collected for market, Buttercup revealed to the workers that, at the very start of the harvest, he had set aside some of the unsellable fruit and used it to brew a vat of apple-and-pear (that's to say pear-and-apple) cider, which had just yielded three large barrels of the stiff drink. One of the barrels would be sold, one would be kept and aged in the farmhouse cellar, but one had been set aside for the fruit-pickers to thank them for all their hard work. He hoped, he said, this would make up for the delay to their wages.

The sheep, alpacas and geckos looked at each other in confusion. None of them could remember Buttercup mentioning a delay to the wages before. The farm provided them with their fodder, but they needed their Manor Pounds to buy any extra comforts. Still, they were all happy to hear about the cider, and decided to withhold their complaints until that was drunk. So the barrels were tapped, the troughs were filled, and the apple-and-pear (that's to say pear-and-apple) cider was enjoyed. Tired muscles eased, shy tongues loosened, and bawdy songs were sung. And by the time the barrel was empty, most of the fruit-pickers had forgotten quite what they had been so determined to complain about in the first place.

That same evening, Martha was late returning to her roost. The gaggle's nesting spots pocked the long grasses beside the drinking pool, which lay a little less than halfway along the path that wound from the farmyard to the quarry. It had kept its ancient name despite the fact few animals had drunk there since a well had been sunk in the farmyard many, many generations ago. As the youngest of the gaggle, and a Brent goose at that, Martha didn't have a prime spot beside the pool, and had to walk a good fifty feet along the reedy, muddy bank to reach her quarters.

When she arrived, she was surprised to find a greylag tail feather, pitch black and iridescent, planted in the middle of her nest. It stood so tall and straight that it could only have been put there on purpose. As she was looking at it, another goose waddled past.

'That's from Duke,' the goose said. Martha thought she heard a certain glee in his voice. 'It's a summons.'

Martha knew Duke by sight, and by reputation, but she'd never spoken to him. He had retired from the gaggle years ago and taken up residence on the uninhabited far side of the drinking pool, just beyond the bounds of Manor Farm. He was known to have been wild-tempered in his day, and was still said to eat the strange vision-causing mushrooms that sometimes sprouted in the spinney.

'What could he want?' Martha asked.

'You're new,' the goose said. 'Perhaps he wants to take you under his wing.' And with a shrill cackle he waddled off to join the others in the shallows.

Martha set off to find Duke. The poolside vegetation grew thicker the further away from the farm she walked, and the separation between water and land became so indistinct that she twice lost her footing and tumbled into the mud. When she finally arrived, Duke was looking across the twilit water through aviator sunglasses, held to his head by a rubber band. In his beak, a cigarette in a long holder loosed thick curls of smoke into the air.

'I got your message,' Martha said.

'What do you see?' Duke said. At first Martha thought he was asking what she saw in front of her, to which she didn't feel she could answer with the truth: a scraggly, balding gander, whose orange beak and legs had faded with age. Then she noticed he was tilting his head towards the distant orchard, where festivities were in full swing.

'A party,' Martha said. 'Fuelled by apple-and-pear cider. Why, what do you see?'

'A fracturing,' Duke said. 'Or a splintering. Not yet. But soon.' While Martha was wondering just how to answer this, Duke turned to her, letting his sunglasses slide down his beak. His eyes were an intense marble black, and shimmered with an almost frightening perceptiveness. 'Apple-and-pear?' he said at last. 'Or pear-and-apple?' It took Martha a moment to realise what the old goose was getting at.

'Oh that!' she said with a shrug. 'Sometimes words change their meaning.'

Duke eyeballed Martha.

'There's a difference between words changing their meaning, and words having their meaning changed,' Duke said. 'Even more so when it's a pig doing the changing.'

'I heard it was the starlings,' Martha said.

'You've got a lot to learn, gosling,' Duke said. His tone irritated Martha. None of the other geese gave Duke the time of day. They treated him as a relic, an eccentric to be ignored. Just because she was polite enough to respond to his summons didn't mean he could talk down to her.

'Apples? Pears? Who cares?' she said. 'Surely this farm has bigger problems than the starlings – or a *pig* – tinkering with a word here or there.'

'You can't *tinker* with reality,' Duke said.

'What do you mean?' Martha asked.

'I mean it's an intricate balance. Look.' Duke gestured at a spider's web. Its taut fibres were glistening in the dying light. When he was sure Martha was looking, he leaned in so that the glowing tip of his cigarette was a hair's breadth away one of the fibres.

'Today, apples and pears,' Duke said. Ash touched fibre and in an instant the whole beautiful web had slumped catastrophically to one side. The old goose turned back to look at Martha. 'And tomorrow?'

OCTOBER

The trees in the spinney turned from deep green to gold and ochre. The sheep and alpacas let their fleeces thicken and the cows started wearing the lighter of their quilted coats. Visiting hours were reduced, and distant bonfires spiced the air at dusk.

Time's invisible wheel continued turning over Manor Farm. The animals might have been forgiven for thinking that it was the farm's windmill, standing on the grassy knoll above the orchard, which drove that wheel forever onwards. For the windmill's sails, affixed atop a brick tower that loomed several times higher than any other building on the farm, were famous far and wide for always turning. Even, some noted, when there was no breeze at all.

The ceaselessness of the windmill meant that it generated enough electricity not only to meet all of Manor Farm's needs, but also to allow Dunning and Kruger – the farm's stocky and cocky bull terriers – to sell its surplus across the Wealden Union and beyond. And yet, despite the windmill's contribution to the farm's coffers, few of the animals had ever sought to understand exactly how it worked, or even climbed the grassy knoll to see it up close. Had they done so, they would have seen that at its base was a heavy door, behind which the magical and secret turbine was locked. The windmill was surrounded by a tall metal fence. It was topped with razor wire to prevent other farms stealing the design. At least, that was what the dogs claimed.

For most of the animals the windmill was just part of the texture of their lives, ever-present like a distant hill or the moon in the sky. Its constant hum was no more disturbing than a light breeze rustling the branches in the spinney, or the lapping of water against the shore of the drinking pool. Which was why none of the animals even noticed when, on the very day that the first leaves began to fall from the trees, the turbine's vanes slowed, creaked, and then stopped turning.

Now that the apple-and-pear harvest was over, and there were fewer visitors to Manor Farm, Cassie finally went to the quarry. On her way there she passed the drinking pool. Martha, the young goose who had told her about the quarry in the first place, was in her ground nest. Only her small, dark head was visible above the rushes. When she saw Cassie plodding past, she nodded at her with encouragement. Cassie nodded back and the goose's eyes seemed to light up.

She had never been to the quarry before, or even beyond the furthest bank of the drinking pool. She had never had any reason. While her ancestors, on both sides, would have regularly trudged the long route to Willingdon market, piled high with the farm's produce, from the time Cassie had reached working age the few things Manor Farm still grew were loaded into a small van, and driven away by one of the more dextrous pigs. Cassie's only regular task was pulling cartloads of visitors around the farmyard, something she tried to accomplish with as much dignity as she could. While she knew her life was certainly less punishing than the lives of all who came before her, she still often wondered which fate she would truly have preferred.

Cassie wasn't sure what she had been expecting from the quarry, but she did know it wasn't what she found. Never in her life had she seen such huge piles of discarded items. She had been expecting something about the size of the rubbish heap behind the cow shed, that had been cleared away several years earlier when the geckos' vivarium was built. Instead, she encountered a vast open pit, several times larger than the farmyard. And almost every inch of its sunken surface was covered. The rusted skeletons of tractors and threshers groped skyward like the remains of a metallic forest. Newspapers tied in bundles with string, some coagulated into solid balls by years of rain and damp, teetered in towers twenty feet tall. Plastic shopping bags, knotted at the handles and knobbled out of shape by whatever was inside, formed a topography of squat, artificial hillocks, while a seemingly endless scree of books and ledgers poured out of overturned cardboard boxes and plastic tubs. There was no life here. No beasts, no fowl, no insects. And no starlings. After a month of their almost constant twittering presence on the farm Cassie felt the heaviness of the silence, like the charge in the air before a thunderstorm.

A path had formed that wound towards the middle of the quarry. Cassie set off along it, unsure where or how she would start her search. And yet start she would. She had wanted to know what had become of her father for as long as she could remember. And for almost as long as that, she had been almost certain that she never would find out. But as her front hooves left the soft earth of the grass bank, and clacked against the stone bed of the quarry, she felt the thinnest jolt of hope that she might finally discover what had happened to that animal who – if Gypsy, Cassie's late mother, was to be believed – had lived through more generations of Manor Farm than any other animal... before one day disappearing without trace.

An hour or so after the mule had plodded past her nest, Martha the goose was startled by the sound of a roaring engine. She took to the sky in time to see a red sports car haring up the loke, its radio turned up loud. The driver was a young, clean-shaven human, with slicked hair and thick-rimmed glasses. He skidded his car to a halt in the gravel and leapt out. He was gangly and thin, except for a very pronounced gut, and was wearing a navy pinstriped suit, a red spotted silk tie and black wingtip brogues. By his side cantered a frisky young beagle carrying a leather briefcase in her mouth.

After pausing to get their bearings, the human and his companion set off towards the farmhouse. Martha watched with interest. Ever since humans had been allowed back on to Manor Farm, they had been prohibited from entering that building. The farmhouse was where the Council of Animals met. It was no place for humans. And yet this human strode up to the door, opened it without knocking, and walked inside.

Martha saw that a number of animals had already gathered in the farmyard. She landed alongside them and listened in to their chatter. They were nervous, but also excited by their conviction that this incursion would now be repelled with considerable force. However, when the door opened again a few moments later, it wasn't the human and his beagle being ejected, but Cosmo, poking his head over the threshold, and catching the attention of one of the pigeons.

'Fly over to the kennels, would you,' he said, somewhat breathlessly. 'And tell Dunning and Kruger that Buttercup would like to see them. At once.'

As Cosmo waited for the bull terriers to swagger through the farmyard, he looked across to the throng which by now included most of the several hundred animals – domestic and wild – on the farm.

'Haw-Haw?' he said, waving a wing at the one gander known to be generously disposed to whoever was First Beast. 'Would you mind joining us too?' Haw-Haw's reaction took Martha aback. At the exact moment of the summons, the gander seemed to puff up with pride, but only for a second. Very quickly, as if realising that he had left his nest unguarded, he turned away from Cosmo. Acting like he hadn't heard him, he waddled off across the farmyard.

As if all this uncommon activity wasn't unsettling enough, the gathered animals heard a key turn in the lock of the farmhouse door as soon as Dunning and Kruger were inside.

'I thought the key to the farmhouse door had been melted down,' Martha heard one hen mutter.

'That's what the mural says!' answered another.

Seconds later, all of the open windows were also slammed one by one, and their curtains yanked shut. Martha noticed an intrepid young starling, with a single white feather on his wing, perch discreetly on the windowsill of the master bedroom. But it was clear from the way he was craning his neck this way and that, that even he was unable to see what was happening inside.

With nothing to do but stare at the walls of the farmhouse, the animals took to speculating about what these strange events might mean. The hens gossiped about the human's car and suit, as well as the fine stitching on the beagle's briefcase. Clive the Bullock told any who would listen that 'I always said this would happen', even though he was unable to say quite what 'this' was. The geckos, as the most recent arrivals on the farm, didn't feel confident enough to express much of an opinion, but made their nervousness clear through their increasingly twitchy movements on the vast east window of the Big Barn. As for the sheep, they paraded various wild theories about the morning's events. The WUF was increasing Manor Farm's contributions, they bleated. Pinchfield was launching a new attempt to annex the far field. The dormice had somehow bankrupted the farm... At first Martha couldn't understand where these theories had come from. They seemed far too complex for these simple ruminants to have come up with by themselves.

Then she noticed something which caused her gizzard to contract. Some of the starlings were dropping out of the flock, alighting on the shoulders of certain sheep, and chirping confidentially into their ears, before taking off and rejoining the others. Martha was aware they could talk, but she had had no idea these birds had started fraternising directly with the groundlings. How long had this been going on? What were they saying? How did they choose which of the animals to talk to? Were they acting alone or on some other animal's orders? And could these starlings somehow be at the root of those outlandish ideas? She felt almost dazed under the barrage of questions she now had.

An hour passed. Two. The farm's gates remained closed to visitors. Morning became afternoon. Afternoon dissolved into dusk. The evening brought a wintry chill but still the animals kept their vigil. Smoke rose from the farmhouse chimney, large flakes of ash dancing in its curlicues. A paper fire must have been lit in the kitchen stove, Martha thought. The starlings were more and more agitated. They had spent most of the day looking on from their hundreds of perches all around the yard, but were now taking to the air in ever greater numbers with ever greater frequency, filling the sky with vast formations that shifted against the twilight like the jerky swirling of a matador's cape.

Finally, as darkness was about to close its fist over Manor Farm, the door of the farmhouse opened and Buttercup emerged. His face was set into a grave expression and he had two dark rings beneath his eyes. Those eyes were fixed on something far off, beyond where the other animals stood. On a future, perhaps, that even his vast pig-brain could no longer control or understand. It was rare for the other pigs not to attend a formal address by the First Beast, but this time Buttercup stood alone. (Although Martha did fancy she saw several of the upstairs curtains twitching as Buttercup spoke.)

'Today,' he said, 'the Council of Animals was visited by a representative of Whymper Associates, the firm through which Dunning and Kruger sell electricity across the county and beyond. As I'm sure you all know, Manor Farm's reliable supply of electricity has long been coveted far and wide. Indeed, demand has outstripped supply for several years, pushing the price to such a level that some farms severely indebted themselves just to keep their supply of it constant. Working hand-in-paw, Whymper and the dogs ingeniously harnessed this demand to sell not only the electricity generated, but also the electricity that would be generated in the days, weeks, months and…' here Buttercup paused and swallowed hard, 'years to come. It was thanks to this market that Manor Farm found the money to repaint the chicken coop, oil the squeaking gate, fix the roof of the farmhouse and construct the Big Barn. It was also thanks to this market that you have all come to know a comfort and leisure that surpassed any experienced by previous generations of animals. Anywhere. The relationship with Whymper Associates dated back decades and until today was at the heart of our success. Until today,' Buttercup repeated these two words solemnly, his voice now creaking with tiredness. 'I will be honest with you,' he said. 'I have always tried to be. And

I hope you always remember that. In recent days there has been a catastrophic… but temporary… collapse in the windmill's output. The precise cause of this collapse is too complicated to get into now, but Dunning and Kruger assure me that they're working night and day to get the sails turning again. Still, several of our largest clients have been spooked by the collapse, and are calling for their future purchases to be refunded. Since the windmill cannot currently provide them with electricity, Manor Farm will have to return their money. Although that is money,' and again Martha noticed Buttercup swallow hard, 'that has, largely, been spent.' Standing in the middle of the mass of animals, now shrouded in almost complete darkness, Martha felt the air thick with confusion and fear. None of them understood how the windmill worked, but all of them understood the consequence of it stopping to do so.

'Thankfully,' Buttercup said, 'Manor Farm is not *entirely* dependent on the windmill for its livelihood. There's the revenue from our visitors, whose numbers have been increasing every season. And there's our produce. Our apples and pears and, if need be, our eggs, wool and milk.

'Wool?' Haw-Haw honked. 'I'm sure the sheep and alpacas will be delighted to surrender their new fleeces, just before winter, and only weeks after working themselves to exhaustion picking fruit!' Buttercup glared at Haw-Haw with such ferocity that the goose's survival instinct kicked in and he dipped his beak in submission.

'What about the Pile?' Clive the Bullock bellowed. 'Why can't we dip into the Pile? Just to get us through the winter?'

'Yes!' joined one of the sheep. 'The Quartermaster said it was for a rainy day!'

These comments were met with a grumble of agreement, although Buttercup seemed not to hear it.

'Be assured,' Buttercup said, 'that, when the time is right, the Council will conduct a full investigation into the causes of this failure. Lessons will be learned. Whymper and the dogs will be reined in. I also give you my word that any extra work… and I'm sorry to say that there *will* be extra work… will be distributed fairly. Now more than ever it is important for us to embody our farm's ancient motto that all animals are more equal than others.'

With that, Buttercup turned on his trotters and walked back into the farmhouse. The last time he had pronounced those words, that night in the Big Barn, they were met with a raucous cheer. Now they were only met with silence.

The animals in the farmyard were stunned. Most of them had not understood half of what Buttercup had said, but they had understood that the collapse of the electricity market would mean more work and less comfort for them all. All? No perhaps not all. It was clear what extra work meant for some of the animals: for the hens a demand to lay more eggs, for the geckos being fondled by even more human children, for Cassie more hours in the bridle. But what did extra work mean for the pigs? Longer days at Council? Surely, Martha thought, Buttercup would not dare suggest this amounted to a comparable sacrifice. And what about Dunning and Kruger? Buttercup had said they would be reined in, but were they to be punished for the recklessness that had caused this crisis? Were their luxurious kennels to be stripped, their studded leather collars and waxed raincoats sold off? No mention had been made of consequences for them at all.

Just then, one of the starlings spotted Cosmo quietly leaving the farmhouse through the coal hatch. Within seconds, several dozen of the flock were causing such a commotion above him that it attracted the attention of the other animals. Clive the Bullock cantered over to the cornered Quartermaster and bellowed in his face:

'Here's your rainy day, owl!'

'As I have explained on many occasions,' Cosmo said, seeming glad to be able to give a rehearsed answer to his tormentors. 'There are issues concerning storage conditions once the silo is open. And besides, the situation is nowhere near critical enough yet that we have to...'

One of the sheep interrupted him.

'If the pigs won't open the silo, I say we do it ourselves!'

Cosmo looked worried.

'That would certainly not be advisa…' he began, before being drowned out by the clamorous agreement of the mobbing beasts. 'You see,' Cosmo tried again once the cheer had subsided. 'Over the years, the abundance and availability of grain in the Pile…'

As he spoke, Martha felt the gathering shift, dragged away from the Quartermaster and towards the silo as if by an irresistible underground force.

'As well as the fact that no animal, from one Council to the next, ever *really* knew how much grain there was because…' Cosmo was now speaking only to the animal's haunches, tails and cloacae as they lumbered, as one many-limbed and many-winged beast, away from the farmhouse and across the farmyard.

'Because, well,' Cosmo loosed a flat chuckle as he scurried after them. 'Who knows how much grain is in a *Pile* anyway?' The first of the animals had already reached the silo, although now they were at their destination, they didn't seem to know what to do.

'The lever!' one of the alpacas bleated, butting her head into an arm of metal, painted red, attached to a small chute at the bottom of the metal container. Clive the Bullock stepped forward and clamped the lever in his immense jaw. He pulled.

'Which is to say, having so much grain available may have proved a little too much temptation for certain pigs of past administrations…'

Cosmo was standing under the chute now, hopping from one foot to the other as Clive strained at the handle beside him. At first it didn't budge. But then slowly, very slowly:

'It's opening!' several of the hens clucked.

And it was. Gradually, rustily, the lever was inching from left to right.

'Not to mention certain dogs,' Cosmo babbled, to no animal but himself. 'And magpies and geese, if my memory serves me correctly…' The lever completed its arc, and the silo released an almighty sound, like the sigh of a slumbering giant finally waking up. The shock of it bumped Cosmo's voice up in pitch, into a barely recognisable warble: 'So the question is, how long can you skim a little off here, a little off there, and yet the Pile remains a Pile? That's a question for the magpies I suppose. All of which is to say that, after a while…'

The silo rumbled. None of the animals were breathing. Some closed their eyes, ready to be swept up, carried away from this promised winter of discomfort on a tide of golden cereal.

'After a while…' Cosmo said, his voice now nothing but dejection, his head cupped in his wing. 'All that was left was…' The rumble subsided. The silo was open, but nothing had come out.

'Empty?' Clive the Bullock murmured in disbelief.

'Not quite,' Cosmo said. And at that moment a single grain, blackened with rot, rolled down the chute, bounced off Cosmo's head and landed – *plunk!* – on the concrete.

Different stories would be told over the troughs of what happened next. Yet, however much the animals disagreed over the manner in which it started, there was no disagreement about the result.

The animals destroyed the sports car. The alpacas kicked in the windows with their hooves, the hens tore out the upholstery with their beaks, the rabbits scratched the paintwork with their claws and teeth, and the sheep cratered the chassis by striking it with their hard foreheads. The pigeons, refusing to let their fragile bodies exclude them, took to flying back and forth until the entire hood was marbled with their droppings. A couple of dormice got inside the engine and nibbled through the brake cables and the fuel line, while a trio of magpies pecked through the clear plastic of the dashboard and stripped the electric wires out with their beaks. And then, when there was little left of the car to destroy, Marguerite and Clive combined their forces to tip it, first on its side, then on its hood. As for the starlings, they had taken to the sky almost as soon as the tumult had begun, but their movements were so chaotic that it was impossible to tell if they supported the destruction of the car or were protesting against it.

Perhaps most surprising of all was the appearance of the pigs Pearl and Dermott in the fray. Pearl was an old member of Buttercup's drove, a relic from a time when 'pigs actually believed in something', as Buttercup himself joked. Dermott was Pearl's young disciple, who refused to fully affiliate himself with the drove due to its abandonment, years earlier, of many of the fundamental tenets of what he called *True* Animalism. Dermott wore an expensively tailored sack coat, and carried the earmark of a common Yorkshire hog, despite clearly being a rare Berkshire stud, bred for exhibition. It was unclear when exactly Pearl and Dermott had arrived at the gathering – by now a riot – but they quickly pushed their way to the middle of things. Except, instead of participating in the violent frenzy, they tried to rouse the other beasts into a rendition of the old hymn 'Animal Farm', bellowing the same two lines over and over in the hope, it seemed, that they would become indelibly associated with the uprising:

> 'Animal Farm, Animal Farm,
> Never through me shall thou come to harm!'

But the tune was slow and turgid compared to 'Beasts of England', and none of the other animals joined in.

The animals were so caught up in the destruction that only Martha saw the back door of the farmhouse open and the man from Whymper, his beagle, as well as Dunning and Kruger, scamper out of the house, vault the dry-stone wall and scurry across the orchard. Before Martha had time to honk a word, they were out of sight.

The commotion only began to subside when the sun turned orange and pendulous, in preparation for its final dive beyond the horizon. The farmyard lights flickered on, and the animals stood and looked upon what they had done with both pride and wonder, but also with a feeling of sadness. For in the midst of their excitement, it had felt as if they were engaged in something that was not destructive but creative, as if their violent actions were somehow tilling the barren earth of their lives. Now the car had been destroyed and their rage had subsided, they were unable to see from where in this wreckage anything new could possibly sprout.

And the damage was not limited to the car. One of the wooden legs of the fodder silo had been splintered, a window of the harness room was cracked, and several of the dustbins had been overturned, their contents strewn across the farmyard and halfway along the loke. Most striking of all was the fact that the words ᴧᴀɴoʀ ᴘoυɴᴅꙅ ꜰoʀ ᴧᴀɴoʀ ᴃꚃᴀꙅᴛꙅ had been daubed in red paint on the glass wall of the Big Barn, completely obscuring the farm's motto. None of the animals present in the farmyard knew who had painted these words, although some of the sheep were quite taken with the phrase, and began bleating it at once, stressing the words 'pounds' and 'beasts' in a way that made them quite hypnotic. But they could not have been responsible. For the words were painted some twenty feet from the ground, and it was well known that sheep could not balance on ladders. Not only was Martha unaware who had painted the words, she was also uncertain what they meant. What was a 'Manor Beast' exactly? She asked one of the sheep, who explained that it simply meant any beast that lived on Manor Farm. Although if this was so, why did some of the geckos and alpacas – whose ancestors had only been here for a few years – feel a little anxious? Even the dormice looked nervously upon the words, and their kind had been resident on Manor Farm for dozens of generations. As the animals stood trying to decipher the meaning of the strange graffiti, Whistler came hopping into the farmyard:

'Did you see?' the magpie cawed. 'Just now, a rock flew out of the yard, right over the paddock, and knocked the starling nest out of the old oak tree? Every one of the eggs smashed!' None of the other animals knew what Whistler was talking about. None of them even knew that before the commotion began there had been a nest with six perfect sky-blue starling eggs lodged in the low bows of the old oak, and so none of them really cared that those eggs had now vanished.

'That sounds like too far for a rock thrown by one of us to have travelled,' Marguerite the Holstein said, scrutinising Whistler through narrowed eyes. 'But if you say it happened, then…'

'I do and it did,' Whistler said. And because it seemed so unimportant when compared to the day's other events, none of the animals saw fit to question Whistler further.

Several days later, Jumbo the pig turned up on Manor Farm. He was dropped at the gate by a sleek black car with tinted windows, which sped off as soon as Jumbo's trotters hit the gravel, almost as if the driver was embarrassed to be seen there. Jumbo had not lived on Manor Farm for several years, but his reputation preceded him, at least among the pigs. He was said to be a liar and a drunkard, perpetually in rut, and to hold a belief in his own right to unlimited pleasure and sensual indulgence. On the day he returned to Manor Farm, Jumbo was overweight, even for a pig. He was scruffily dressed in an ill-fitting business suit, his short, bristly fur was unkempt and matted and his snout was caked with dried food and stained with red wine. Wine wasn't common on Manor Farm, where beer was preferred, but flowed freely in the taproom of the Red Lion, the gastro-pub in Willingdon where the WUF met. Jumbo was also wearing a jet-black human hairpiece which sat catastrophically upon his flat head.

For the past few years Jumbo had been a member of the Jonesist delegation to the Wealden Union of Farmers. Since the Jonesists had not won a Choozin for more than six years, any presence they had at the WUF was largely symbolic. That was why it was suspected that Jumbo had been sent there in the hope of limiting the trouble he could cause on Manor Farm, and as a subtle slight to an organisation the Jonesists resented. And yet, while these days few of the animals gave much thought to the WUF one way or the other – apart from a handful of Ribbons's more traditionalist pigs who would never, *could* never, accept the possibility that Foxwood and Pinchfield were friends, one thing everyone knew was that Jumbo was there, upsetting the pear cart whenever he could.

He trotted up the loke, across the farmyard, stopped to look quizzically at the starlings for a moment, and walked into the farmhouse. He climbed the stairs to the first floor, where the Jonesists met. There, he dropped his suitcase onto the rug, slumped into the old chaise-longue, and greeted Ribbons with an inscrutable grin.

'What happened now?' the stunned Ribbons asked him. Jumbo chuckled.

'How much time have you got?' he said. Several of the other Jonesist pigs laughed at this, and Ribbons shot them a scolding glare. 'I'm teasing!' Jumbo said. He took a pear from his pocket and bit down into it. 'It just felt like a good time to come back.'

Ribbons was so unsettled by the troublesome pig's return that he didn't notice his old rival Curly, standing in the corner of the room, tapping his circular slide-rule against his snout, and scrutinising Jumbo with great interest.

NOVEMBER

As Autumn turned into winter on Manor Farm, the admission price was slashed, bringing in more visitors. For the first time in many years the hens' eggs and the wool from the sheep and alpacas were sold off. A buyer was even sought for the milk from the cows, an indignity to which Marguerite the Holstein had never again expected her species to be subjected. Life became harder than at any other time the animals could remember.

Even though none of them, except the dogs, and perhaps the pigs, were to blame for the downturn in the farm's fortunes, all of them were working more. Except for the dogs, and perhaps the pigs. At first, the pigs were very fond of informing the other animals of each and every sacrifice they themselves made, although most of these seemed related to the number of 'files' they now had to deal with. Since few of the other animals had any idea what a 'file' was, this did not garner much sympathy, particularly after a day strapped into the milking machine, being fondled by human children, or clearing up their parents' litter. So after a while the pigs learned to keep their complaints to themselves.

The animals often spoke about the 'Whopping Commotion', as that glorious day they had destroyed the red sports car had quickly become known, uttering it with the same overripe reverence they had previously reserved for the 'Great Rebellion' and the 'First Choozin'. Although the precise details of what had happened changed depending upon which animals were talking. Listening to the sheep, anyone would believe it was an entirely ovine affair, a telling that Marguerite, who was slightly embarrassed by the cows' involvement, was happy to encourage. Indeed whenever the Whopping Commotion was mentioned, Marguerite would shake her head sadly and mutter something about the worrying decline in sheeply manners. For the pigeons, it was the weight of their droppings that had crumpled the car's hood, while the magpies recalled the crucial moment as being when they had rewired the car's electrics so that the internal combustion engine had exploded. As for Pearl and Dermott, their telling recalled the Whopping Commotion not as a spontaneous outburst of bestial anger, but as a conscious and determined uprising in the name of True Animalism. It sometimes seemed as if there were as many tellings as there were participants. Each of these tellings was held to be true by at least some of the animals, while certain among them had no difficulty believing several tellings at once.

What about the graffiti? At first Buttercup had declared that it would be removed and the farm's motto restored to its former prominence on the window of the Big Barn. However, since the removal of paint required labour and money, which the farm could not currently spare; since it might not be particularly expedient, given the current situation, to remind the animals of Manor Farm's commitment to equality; and since the sheep had taken the phrase 'MANOR POUNDS FOR MANOR BEASTS' to heart and had started seeking forces outside of the farm to blame for the current difficulties, Buttercup decided to delay the removal of the paint until things had settled down and life on the farm had returned to normal.

As winter's jaw closed over the farm, the impact of the starlings upon life only increased. There were more and more of them in the farmyard. When they were at rest, no fence post, chimney pot or drainpipe sat empty, while every inch of gutter and dry-stone wall was filled with its own tight rank of glistening midnight-blue lodgers, and every hedgerow was raucous with their trill.

Martha was starting to feel a profound unease about the effects the flock were having on the farm. When the starlings had first arrived she felt she was not alone in asking certain questions – Where had they come from? What did they want from Manor Farm? Who had sent them… and why? There had been no more mention from Buttercup about getting rid of them. And for most of the animals, familiarity with the flock had seemingly bred acquiescence. Martha had noticed more and more of them letting one starling after another alight on their shoulders and gossip into their ears for minutes on end, and yet none of them seemed to pay any attention to the flock as a whole these days. A flock whose constant watchful presence she was starting to find a little menacing, particularly when combined with the suspicion that they might collectively know more about life on the farm than the animals knew themselves. Only Whistler the magpie seemed to be watching them with the same intensity as Martha. She had several times spotted him observing the starlings, a short pencil pinched tight in his beak and an exercise book on the ground in front of him, which he held open by his burnt-twig feet, as he sketched off one diagram after another. But as soon as Whistler saw Martha watching him, he'd flip his book closed and drag it away and out of her sight.

Perhaps the animals had come to accept the starlings because many of their actions seemed harmless, intended – if there were any intent – to encourage an atmosphere of merriment and camaraderie amid the recent gloom. Like the time several dozen of them prevented a visitor from returning to his car by surrounding him with a whirling wall of wings. Martha had earlier watched this man insist his brattish, shrill-voiced daughter be allowed to ride one of the alpacas, responding to her cries of 'But *Daaah-Deee!*' as if they were edicts handed down by one of those spiritual rulers the humans seemed so keen on. Although she had also seen the muck his family had left sprawled across the picnic tables, so couldn't be sure for which misdeed the starlings were punishing him. Either way, it was clear many of the animals felt heartened by such immediate and mischievous payback.

There were also times, however, when the starlings' behaviour appeared strikingly scolding. So much so that Martha suspected some of the animals were changing their behaviour to avoid any reprisal. Balmoral, the stuffy old roe stag, had been chased from the yard merely for uttering his ridiculous idea – which he had been loudly advocating year in year out for as long as Martha could remember – that a deep, defensive moat should be dug around the farm. Since then Martha had heard him using uncharacteristically mild language whenever he raised the subject. Could this really be because of his treatment by those birds? And what had happened to that sheep that the starlings had repeatedly dive-bombed until she tried to flee and got stuck in the old cattle-grid at the top of the loke, all because she'd snuck back to the trough for an extra feed? Martha had seen neither hide nor hair of her since that day.

Martha also suspected the starlings were responsible, in part at least, for the change that had come over Haw-Haw. Ever since the day of the Whopping Commotion, when he had rejected the summons from Buttercup, Haw-Haw's waddle had become more of a swagger. He had always been a goose of strident views but had also been as dedicated as the rest of the gaggle to reporting farm events not as he saw them, but as they were and then, as custom dictated, only when asked to do so by one of the other animals. Now he'd honk as he made his way around the farmyard, giving his opinion (and nothing but his opinion) to any animal within earshot. Which, considering the excellent hearing many of the animals had, meant few were spared his thoughts:

'Buttercup's Bad Management the Source of Manor Farm's Woes!'

'First Beast's Faulty Vision Means Winter of Hardship for All!'

Martha found him truculent and annoying… and yet how popular Haw-Haw now was! Among the sheep, alpacas and cows in particular, but also among the rats, rabbits and pigeons, who found this new style of goose far more entertaining. Even gangs of the starlings were stirred into a frenzy above the farmyard whenever Haw-Haw spoke.

Despite all of her apprehension, when the starlings took to the air, Martha was as transfixed as all the others for the short duration of their performances. Pig, horse, sheep, gecko, dormouse, alpaca, cow and goose all gawped skyward with a mix of confusion, delight and awe. Only the pigeons didn't watch. They, instead, took to their loft at the first sign of movement from their shiny feathered cousins.

Then, on a moonlit night several weeks after the Whopping Commotion, Martha was visited in her nest by a starling. It was the bird with the single white wing feather she had first noticed perched on an upstairs windowsill of the farmhouse, trying to see what was happening inside.

The young bird landed on a reed, its negligible weight barely causing the slender leaf to dip, and began hopping from one foot to the other, waiting for the goose to say something. Martha was put in mind of how upset human children appeared as they queued, impatiently, to use the visitor toilets (a peculiar quirk no animal could understand) so decided to end the starling's misery.

'Martha,' she said offering her wing.

'Scout!' the visitor peeped.

'Can I... help you, Scout?' Martha asked.

'Magpie! Last night! Flying back to the farm! Whistler!' Scout chirruped.

'Whistler?' Martha said. 'Flying? That's impossible.' Every animal knew that it had been several generations since any of Manor Farm's magpies had flown, thanks to a compromise with the Council dating back to Traviata's day. Since the magpies had brains to rival the pigs', the Council considered it unfair, and even dangerous, that the birds should also be able to achieve the added vantage that the gift of flight gave them. So Traviata had proposed housing the magpies in comfort in the harness room, on the condition they submit to having their wings clipped. The magpies had resisted at first, but came round to Traviata's way of thinking when they saw the buckets of grubs and berries she had arranged for them. These buckets had diminished over the years, but by then the magpies had completely lost their instinct for scavenging and their taste for flight.

'And yet!' Scout said. 'Happened!'

Martha had never been so close to a starling before, or alone with one, and was struck by how agitated, almost fevered, this one seemed. He also spoke in high-pitched staccato bursts, as if he existed on a different temporal plane, and was struggling to adapt to the sluggish pace at which the ground-based animals lived.

'Why are you telling me?' Martha began.

'More!' Scout interrupted. 'Not flying alone!'

Martha decided not to push her question, but just to let Scout speak. She nodded for him to go on. The starling couldn't keep still as he spoke. One moment he was on the reed in front of Martha, the next he was atop a waterlogged fence post several yards behind. Then he was hovering inches from Martha's face, and then was nowhere to be seen… before reappearing on the reed once more. Martha found the whole exchange confusing and hard to concentrate on, but was just about able to piece together a story.

It seemed that Whistler had glided over Manor Farm at the head of a V-shaped formation of newly fledged starlings. The young birds were as fixated on the magpie as if he was their mother. As Scout told it, this strange flight circled the farmhouse twice, before landing in the deserted yard. Then, peering around to check he wasn't being watched, Whistler made the birds climb one-by-one onto his wingtip and flicked them into the air. After they had found their perches around the farmyard, all seven of Whistler's starlings became entirely indistinguishable from the rest of the sleeping flock.

After such strange behaviour, Scout determined to keep an eye on Whistler, and followed him to the front door of the farmhouse first thing the following morning. The magpie was seeking an urgent audience with either Buttercup or Ribbons. Neither pig deigned to receive the scraggly corvid. He then began a vigil on the rail of the porch, petitioning every pig that came and went for a moment of their valuable time. It wasn't until late in the afternoon that one pig accepted: Curly the squashed-faced Baston. He was about to ignore Whistler, just like all the others, when something the magpie said stopped him dead. He turned, the two of them spoke with uncommon intensity, and Curly invited Whistler inside.

'What did he say?' Martha asked, surprised by the force of her own curiosity. 'Why did he change his mind?' Scout took to the air, and began turning tight, jittery circles around Martha's head.

'Don't know! Couldn't hear!' he said. 'Sorry!' before shooting off over the hedgerows in a breakneck bouncing corkscrew.

DECEMBER

The days grew colder, visitor numbers dwindled again, and Cassie the mule's rickety old cart was locked away. This happened every winter, although the difference this year was that – 'in line with the farm's cost-saving efforts' as Cosmo had put it – Cassie's hay ration was cut because she would be expending less energy 'in service of the farm'. Since they had never increased her rations during the summer months, when the number of rides she gave would often double, Cassie felt this new rule quite unfair. And yet, as was her way, she didn't grumble. She had never had a huge appetite, and the extra idle hours meant that for the past several weeks she had been able to visit the quarry almost every day. Not that she had found anything of interest among the rusting heaps of empty tin cans, several dozen volumes of *The British Almanac*, warped by the damp, and pile after pile of unsold *30 Glorious Years Since the Great Rebellion* mugs, tee shirts and plush toys.

One crisp morning, as Cassie passed the drinking pool, she veered off the gravel path that led to the quarry, and instead made her way towards the reed beds where the geese roosted. She wanted to speak to the young fowl who had first recommended she root around among decades of Manor Farm's rubbish. Perhaps she needed some kind of reassurance that she wasn't wasting her time.

Martha wasn't in her nest – a homely if rickety construction of twigs, leaves, mosses and down, which sat in a depression in the ground, not far from the shore – but instead perched on top of a high tree stump, scrutinising the farmyard from afar. Cassie turned to see what she was looking at, but from this distance only had a blurry sense of the activity below. Despite being quietly proud of her own excellent eyesight – which she knew to be much better than the pigs' at least – Cassie was a little surprised that this goose could not only see what was happening in the yard but apparently hear it too.

'It's like this every day now, from dawn till dusk,' Martha said.

'Like what?' Cassie asked.

'Haven't you noticed how it's become almost impossible to cross the farmyard without being barracked by some pig or goose?' Martha said. 'Up on their pear crates, honking or grunting some new wild notion about what *really* caused the windmill to stop turning, or where all the farm's money *actually* went…'

Cassie hadn't spent much time in the farmyard recently, but she certainly agreed that something had changed since the day of the Whopping Commotion. It was as if the mixture of fear and exhaustion had stirred the animals from a long sleep. Only they had woken into a shifting, fragmented world in which they had no bearings. Or perhaps they were just hungry. Either way, it did feel that they were longing for someone new to come along, someone new with new answers… and apparently there was no dearth of animals, pigs mostly, willing to be that someone.

'There's definitely something in the air,' Cassie said.

'Apart from the starlings, you mean?' Martha replied, nodding in the direction of the vast murmuration that had just then taken to the sky for its morning manoeuvres. Against the blue, the mass of birds formed a ball, then a huge flat plate, and then – blink and you'd have missed it – what looked to Cassie like the shape of a pig's head. Cassie had been caught off guard by Martha's remark, and then by the realisation of how little mind she had paid to the starlings these past months, most likely because none of them ever made it as far as the quarry.

'Do you think the starlings have something to do with the new mood in the farmyard?' Cassie asked.

'That's precisely what I'm trying to understand,' Martha said.

Cassie liked this young bird. She was normally not too fond of geese. She found them too excitable, too quick to have an opinion and to share that opinion with the whole world. Her maternal cart horse roots meant Cassie's mind was slow but stolid. She could also be profoundly stubborn, and sceptical almost to the point of world-weariness. This she had inherited from her father – at least as her mother Gypsy told it. All of which made talking with geese quite tiresome. But she sensed a rare honesty and thoughtfulness to Martha.

'Do you think the Council will put a stop to it?' she asked.

'They've tried,' Martha said. 'They banned pear crates from the farmyard during opening hours, by claiming they were putting off visitors at a time when Manor Farm needed them most. But I suspect that the *real* reason is that Buttercup and Ribbons are often their target. Most of them aren't affiliated with either Animalist nor Jonesist, you see. It doesn't matter, anyway, because nobody is paying any attention to the rule, and…' Martha stopped talking suddenly, and tilted her head at Cassie. 'I have some crackers if you want them?'

At first Cassie didn't understand what Martha meant. Then she realised that, while Martha had been talking, she had been chewing on one of the thick and bitter reeds that spiked up all along the banks of the drinking pool. Martha hopped down from the tree stump, rustled about in her nest and turned up a plastic tube of savoury biscuits.

'They fell out of a human's bag, which I know isn't ideal, but don't look a gift… I mean, don't turn your nose up at a gift, right? Anyway, if you'd…'

'Yes,' Cassie said, spitting out the half-chewed reed. 'Yes, please.'

Late one afternoon in the middle of December, Buttercup summoned Cosmo to the Big Barn's gallery. When he arrived Buttercup invited him to sit in one of two wicker rocking chairs, which he'd arranged to look out over the floor below.

'What do you see?' the First Beast asked Cosmo.

The owl looked out across the room. It was a hive of activity. That night was to be the final pear-bobbing before the farm closed for the winter solstice. Coloured lanterns were being hung from every wall and the troughs were being filled with spiced cider. It was a more sombre effort than previous years, with fewer decorations, but it cheered Cosmo all the same. He knew that Buttercup wasn't talking about the celebrations. Along the walls of the Big Barn, half a dozen pigs were standing on upturned pear crates, each surrounded by groups of animals. The pigs were hectoring their audiences, and the animals were responding with cheers or heckles. Buttercup clearly felt he had waited long enough for Cosmo to reply, because he spoke again.

'I see ingratitude,' he said again. 'After everything I've done for them.'

They watched in melancholy silence as one unaffiliated pig after another spoke out against the Council of Animals:

'Who is Buttercup to tell you how to spend your hard-earned Manor Pounds?' snorted one pig.

'If you believe that we're safer from Foxwood and Pinchfield now we've removed the barbed-wire fences, then I've got a broken windmill to sell you!' shouted a second.

'The starlings are an omen!' squealed a third. 'The plague to end all plagues is coming!'

'Ask yourselves this: will your chicks, and calves, and lambs, and crias live better or worse lives than you?' lamented a fourth.

There was a flurry of activity and a movement among the animals to one side of the room. Even some of the starlings, a few hundred perhaps, had abandoned their dusk manoeuvres, swarmed into the Big Barn, and were circling in the eaves looking for somewhere to perch.

'I've even lost the farmyard Set,' Buttercup said. He was talking about those young beasts in the crowd who'd migrated from the outer fields to the farmyard, rejecting the traditional lives of sheep, or rabbit, or hen, or dormouse, to take up roles as cashiers, tour guides, or waiters. Some worked for the Council or the dogs, or crafted the trinkets that were sold to visiting humans. Buttercup felt that he was responsible for the creation of this group, certainly for their enrichment – and yet now they had turned against him even more determinedly than the rest.

The enthusiasm was not being stirred by some young pig, but by Pearl, the old Animalist tub-thumper, who was now mounting his pear crate, his signature black sack coat draped over his arthritic shoulders. The animals at the front of the crowd welcomed him as a prophet, while those a little further back looked on more with curiosity than admiration.

'Fellow animals!' Pearl squealed, his voice cracking with the strain. 'For too long Buttercup has told us the lie that things cannot be better. That there is no alternative. That an animal's life is only the windmill, and the Big Barn's gift shop, and the WUF... and nothing more.' The old pig succumbed to a fit of coughing. He held up a trotter while he tried to gather himself.

'He speaks as if I'm the enemy,' Buttercup whispered to Cosmo. 'As if Ribbons and Traviata never existed.'

'Why do you put up with it?' Cosmo asked.

'I'd have been a fool not to keep him in the drove,' Buttercup said. 'He's far more dangerous outside than in. I'd never be mad enough to kick him out. Besides Pearl's just a cured carcass trained by Dermott to grunt a handful of catchy slogans.'

'Dermott? His assistant?' Cosmo said. Buttercup smiled thinly at the description.

'Did you know that he's been spreading the rumour that I made a lot of money when the windmill stopped? That I keep it hidden somewhere on Manor Farm? He thinks most of the animals here are too stupid to understand their game.'

Pearl had caught his breath now:

'But I'm here to tell you another life is possible, my fellow animals. Do you believe in a place where it is Sunday seven days a week?'

'We do!' The cry went up from the knot of supporters at the front of the crowd. Among them Cosmo spotted Flaxen from the snooty roe deer herd that lived at the far end of the orchard. She was wearing a headscarf, and had a silhouette of Pearl's face stencilled on her flank.

'Do you believe in a place where clover is in season all year round?' Pearl went on.

'We do!' More of the crowd joined in this time. The thread-bare legend of evergreen clover, while scientifically absurd, was popular nevertheless.

'Do you believe in a place where lump sugar and linseed cake grows in the hedges?'

'We do!' Now almost all of the gathered animals had chimed in.

'And what is that place called?' A few of the animals at the back of the crowd, who were listening to Pearl for the first time, hollered what they thought was the answer – 'Manor Farm!' – but they were drowned out by the more vociferous supporters at the front:

'Sugarcandy Mountain!'

Buttercup and Cosmo exchanged a glance of disbelief.

'Sugarcandy Mountain,' Pearl repeated, a beatific look in his rheumy eyes. 'And I've come to tell you the good news. Sugarcandy Mountain is here! We just need to dig for it!'

Dermott now handed Pearl a shovel which he waved frantically above his head. Several of the other animals in the crowd waved their own shovels too.

'Ex... Excuse me?' A young ewe, about halfway back had raised her hoof, attempting to attract Pearl's attention. The old pig looked confused. He wasn't used to fielding questions during his speeches. Still, he nodded for the sheep to speak. 'I'm sorry,' she said. 'But... how exactly do we dig for a mountain?' The crowd greeted this question with an exasperated sigh. As if the naïve sheep was the only one present who hadn't done her homework.

'And can't we have these things... *without* digging for Sugarcandy Mountain?' she pushed on. 'It seems like such a terrible waste of energy.'

This time the animals at the front of the crowd erupted in mirth: 'What rot!', 'So gullible!', 'Dumb woolyback!' While a flank of several dozen starlings swooped down from the eaves forming a kind whirlwind around the poor sheep's head, until she was forced to scamper out the barn. Pearl just shook his head, sadly.

'Would that it were possible,' he said. 'But history has taught us that the only way to achieve abundance for all is by following the path of True Animalism. And that path leads, *inevitably*, to Sugarcandy Mountain.' The crowd cheered again. Cosmo saw a flash of envy in Buttercup's eyes. There was a time when he had been similarly loved.

'The same old chestnuts,' Buttercup said, coldly.

'They believe in something,' Cosmo said.

'But it's nonsense.'

'But it's *something*,' Cosmo said. Buttercup shook his head.

'If Pearl ever becomes First Pig, I'd give us five years before the whole farm is sold off, stripped for scrap by Foxwood and Pinchfield.'

'First *Beast*,' Cosmo corrected Buttercup, although his boss seemed not to hear. They watched as the crowd of animals surrounded Pearl now, lifted him over their heads and carried him aloft from the Big Barn. So loud were the cheers from the crowd, that neither Buttercup nor Cosmo heard the dull thud of a tape recorder, secreted beneath the boards of the gallery, spooling to a stop.

Anew crowd started amassing. This was the pear-bobbing audience. Pear (that's to say apple) bobbing was an early innovation after Buttercup's first Choozin victory, and had since become an institution cherished by animals from the hayfield to the spinney. The game was simple: animals bought tickets in the hope of winning a week free from toil if the fruit carved with their number was yanked from the water-filled barrel by the 'bobber's' teeth. The pear-bobbing was chaotic and fun, and attracted animals of every kind to the Big Barn, although most of the numbered tickets were snapped up by the sheep, alpacas and hens, for whom a week of rest meant respite from the drudgery of their lives. It was a prize that had grown in value these last few months. Martha had never bought a ticket. She didn't think of what she did as 'toil' and, besides, didn't want a week off. Like many others, she came every Sunday for the simple fun of the spectacle, as well as what it taught her about the other animals' lives.

Once the bobbing barrel had been rolled into place and filled to the brim with water, Rocky, the ginger tom with the bright pink nose, was welcomed with a rowdy cheer. His tiny, sequined tuxedo glistened under the lights as he sprung onto the raised platform. He grinned at the crowd, then licked each of his paws in turn, and dragged them over his flat forehead, grooming the fur there into a jaunty crest. Then he approached the microphone of the farm's public address system, which ensured his reedy call would be heard above the raucous crowd.

'Good evening, you dirty beasts!' he mewled. The animals cheered again. 'We've got a very special bobber lined up for you this evening. For the first time ever, a *pig* will be getting his snout wet!' A coo of surprise rippled around the Big Barn. Martha startled from her daydream. A pig? This was new. While the pigs often attended the bobbing, she couldn't believe that one of them would submit to the indignity of the sport itself. Rocky went on:

'So please give the warmest of Big Barn welcomes to tonight's bobber, recently back from the WUF, it's the one, the only... Jumbo!' Another gasp as Jumbo emerged from the shadows and began lumbering up the steps to the raised platform.

Jumbo. Of course! Ever since the troublesome boar had been spotted on the farm, many of the geese could talk about little else, at least among themselves. Of particular interest was precisely why he had been forced to return from Willingdon. The rumour was that Jumbo, drunk on red wine after cavorting with the humans, geese and other pigs at the Red Lion, had got his head trapped in the window of the pub's outhouse, apparently while trying to catch a glimpse of a particularly attractive sow as she passed water. The landlord had been forced to pry the metal window frame loose from the wooden boards just to free him, and then Jumbo had had no choice but to wear it, like a geometric necklace, for the entire afternoon, until a blacksmith could be summoned to cut him free. Martha didn't know if the story was true, and none of the geese, not even Haw-Haw, dared spread it about the farmyard without some kind of evidence.

It was the role of the previous week's winner to drop the pears into the water. Lionel, a young honey-coloured alpaca, was ushered onto the stage. Jumbo looked at Lionel through narrowed eyes as he emptied the bucket of pears, each carved with a different number, into the barrel. Then he leaned into Rocky's microphone:

'Oh, he's an alpaca!' Jumbo said. 'I thought for a minute he was a sheep who'd got his head stuck in a mangle!' The alpacas were sensitive about their long necks and several of them expressed their upset by chewing and spitting furiously. The sheep bleated with delight at the joke, which only angered the alpacas further. Rocky frowned. Not only did he object to the cruel remark, he wasn't used to being upstaged. He took the microphone.

'You'd know about getting your head stuck of course,' he said, nudging Jumbo. 'I mean, we all know about what happened at the Red Lion.'

The audience of animals gasped again. This time at Rocky's nerve. The rumour was out then, Martha thought. But how? Jumbo's face contorted into a rictus grin, but there was a flash of fury in his eyes.

'Shall we get on with it?' he said, shoving past Rocky and stepping behind the barrel.

'In your own time,' Rocky replied, devilishly pleased with himself.

Jumbo took a deep breath, rested his trotters on the rim of the barrel and plunged his head under the water. The gathered animals cheered and clutched their tickets. Five seconds Jumbo was under. Ten. Twenty. And then with a heave and a grunt his head came out. The hairpiece was still miraculously in place, and between his teeth sat a glistening, round, Granny Smith pear. Rocky held out his hand to receive it, but Jumbo spat it onto the platform.

'There's one!' he said. Then, before Rocky could even stoop to pick it up, the pig had plunged his head into the barrel again, withdrawing much quicker this time with a second pear in his mouth. Then a third. Then a fourth.

'What are you doing?' Rocky looked startled, his tail stiff and bristling. 'There can be only one winner!' This was the agreement Rocky had struck with Buttercup when they'd come up with the idea for the pear-bobbing. One animal could have one week off.

Any more than that would be far too expensive for the farm. Particularly now.

'I don't know,' Jumbo said, his grin much less forced now. 'Just one winner seems a little ungenerous, wouldn't you say? I think all these good Manor Beasts deserve the whole week off.' And with that, Jumbo turned and gave the barrel a determined kick with his hind trotter. It teetered, and for a moment looked like it might not fall. Martha felt as if time itself had slowed down almost to a stop as she and all the other animals present waited to know which way it would tip. A dozen starlings swooped down from the eaves and landed on the barrel's rim. Their tiny weight was just enough to prove decisive. It fell, and a cascade of water and pears surged over the crowd.

The sheep and alpacas broke into savage bouts of cheering, celebrating what surely had to mean a week's holiday for them all. The hens, who hated getting wet, were shrieking. Rocky sat slumped on the raised platform, a look of utter dismay on his face. Ribbons, who Martha only then realised had been watching from the back of the Big Barn, barged his way out, muttering something about how it was beneath a Jonesist to court the 'deplorable mutton'. Above them all, hundreds of starlings were racing furiously around beneath the rafters. Indeed, things were so chaotic that nobody except Martha noticed Jumbo take his leave, slipping out of the rear door of the Big Barn, closely followed by Curly the Baston pig.

The next morning Martha found another shiny black feather planted in her nest. Duke. When she arrived on the far side of the drinking pool, he was in an agitated mood, waddling back and forth on the same few feet of shoreline. He looked as if he hadn't slept for several days, and was scrawnier than on her first visit, although no less full of tensile energy.

'You know that compass we've all got buried in our heads? The one that's tuned in to the magnetic poles and that helps us get around?' Duke said.

'Yes,' Martha said. 'I think so.' That sense of orientation was so instinctive to Martha that she hadn't ever really given it much thought.

'Well, my compass…' Duke said. He paused to draw slowly and deeply on the cigarette. It turned into a horizontal column of ash that hung there for a second before dropping into the water with a hiss. 'Is tuned in to something quite different.'

'I don't understand,' Martha said.

'I get these hunches,' Duke said. 'Sometimes they're visions, sometimes words. They're normally worth sussing out. Except…' He tailed off.

'Except?' Martha asked.

'Except, I'm getting a little old to do the sussing myself.'

Martha's heart leapt almost into her mouth. So Duke did want to take her under his wing. She felt a mix of fear and pride which she tried to keep from her voice. The other geese may mock Duke when he wasn't around, but Martha sensed they all knew that his instinct for snuffling out a story had once been second to none.

'What's your latest… hunch?'

Duke leaned slowly forward until his nose was touching the mud. Martha didn't know what to do. Was he passing out?

Then, very quickly and deliberately he drew a line in the mud.

He straightened up, looked Martha straight in the eye:

'You. Are. What. You. Eat.'

'And what does that mean?'

'If I knew, I wouldn't have planted that feather in your nest. I'm not asking you to do any sussing right now, just keep it in mind.'

'We're geese,' Martha said. 'We eat roots, shoots and seeds.'

Duke laughed.

'Pry on, you crazy gosling,' he said, and turned back to the pool.

Back on the near side of the drinking pool, Martha saw two of the older greylags cleaning themselves. It was a meticulous process, pulling dirt off their feathers, one by one, with the ridges on their mandibles. At first Martha had been surprised at the diligence with which the notoriously lazy domesticated geese carried out the procedure, until she'd understood that these grooming sessions gave them the chance to share stories with each other and to gossip. And nothing was more important to a goose than gossip. As a bit of an oddity in the gaggle, as well as one of the youngest, Martha had not yet been asked to join a grooming session herself, and so often forgot to clean her own feathers. She was quite sure Duke hadn't cleaned his for years. It was with a certain apprehension, then, that she approached the greylags and asked if she could speak with them about Duke.

'That old crank?' one of them said.

'What news from the far side?' asked the other. Martha could tell they didn't take Duke seriously, and felt worried, suddenly, that this judgement might rub off on her.

'He said he had a hunch,' Martha tried.

'I bet he did!' said the first goose.

'When does he not?' asked the second.

'And then he drew a line in the mud with his beak,' Martha went on.

'That sounds like him,' said the first.

'What kind of line?' asked the second.

'Well, it was more of a squiggle I suppose.'

'The plot thickens!' said the first.

'Which was it?' asked the second. 'A line, or a squiggle?'

'Either way it sounds very important,' said the first.

'Doesn't it?' said the second.

Martha felt a rising sense of panic. They weren't just mocking Duke, they were mocking her too. If she wasn't careful she might lose the respect of the gaggle... before she'd even had a chance to win it. The first goose looked suddenly pensive.

'Then again, he did foresee Traviata getting driven out of office.'

'And didn't he warn us about the great storm of twenty-seven?'

'He did, he did.' The two geese turned away from each other and looked out across the water for a few seconds in silence.

'Though you know what they say,' said the second eventually. The first goose's eyes lit up.

'That a goose on the wing with a dicky tummy...'

'Will always eventually poop on the farmer's head.'

At which the pair of them broke out into such a fit of sardonic honking that Martha turned and beat a retreat to her nest.

Later that day the Council announced that, despite Jumbo's actions, it was impossible for all of the pear-bobbing ticket-holders to have the week off. So that no animal should be treated unfairly, it was instead decided that there would be no winner. Furthermore, until safeguards could be brought in to ensure no similar fiascos could occur in future, the pear-bobbing itself would be put on an indefinite hiatus.

All week, whenever Rocky and Buttercup were seen, the sheep rushed to heckle them:

'Fibbers!'

'No better than humans!'

'Taking the linseed cake from the mouths of lambs!'

And yet, when Jumbo crossed the farmyard he was entirely spared the sheep's ire.

JANUARY

Early in the new year, a flock of cleaning pigeons discovered a small pile of bullet-shaped droppings behind the Big Barn. On the following morning, slashes were found in the faux leather benches of the picnic tables behind the vivarium. Both discoveries pointed to the presence of a fox. But these creatures had been banned from Manor Farm for decades; ever since Edwina, the farm's resident vixen, had been run off the estate after colluding with Pilkington to annex the far field. And yet, as the days passed the evidence piled up: Moulted red fur was found on the sofas in the visitor area, the bins behind the Big Barn were tipped over and their contents scattered, and the hens started noticing a musky stench coming from wet patches of ground near their coop. The frightened dormice gathered the hens and pigeons together to encourage the Council of Animals to act. It was essential, they said, that the Council take steps to scare off this intruder before it took up permanent residence on the farm and made their lives a misery, just as it had done for their ancestors. Cosmo was sent out onto the porch to meet them. He hopped onto the back of the rocking chair, blinked a few times to accustom his eyes to the daylight, and spoke: 'The evidence as we see it does not yet, reasonably, point to the definitive presence of a fox. Any animal, indeed any *number* of animals, could be responsible for the droppings and fur. Still, the Council gives its word that foxes will *never* return to Manor Farm. At least, not on Buttercup's watch.'

The first sightings came a few days later. Early one morning, an alpaca got a fright when he saw a svelte form sprinting through the orchard and, about a week after that, the same red creature was seen squatting and defecating near the windmill. The next night, the hens were woken by a harsh screeching sound and were terrified to find themselves looking straight into the green eyes of a russet-furred, pointy-nosed beast trailing its thick claws menacingly across the viewing window of their coop.

Again the dormice, hens and pigeons appealed to the Council, and again Cosmo came out onto the porch to tell them no action would be taken.

'From a distance,' Cosmo said, 'a stoat, ferret, otter, or any of the other *harmless* wild animals that enjoy free passage across Manor Farm, might reasonably be mistaken for a fox.'

'What about the intruder at the hen's coop?' one of the dormice asked. Cosmo thought about this for a moment before replying:

'I admit that, at first, this might seem like a decisive sighting. But it must also be remembered that none of you have ever seen a *Wealden* fox. Thanks, largely, to Buttercup's prodigious success in repelling them.' The animals exchanged uncertain looks. Cosmo went on: 'While it is of course unacceptable that *any* beast menace the hens, to lay the responsibility on a fox seems to be an unhelpful overreaction.'

Despairing of the Council's response, the dormice, hens and pigeons turned to the geese, but were met with similar dismissiveness from Haw-Haw:

'Don't you think that if a fox had returned, us geese would not only be aware of it but would be honking it from the rooftops?' he said.

And so a strange kind of inactivity took hold, with most of the animals convinced that a fox had returned to Manor Farm, but with the pigs and geese unconvinced that the current sightings were solid enough grounds upon which to take action. And although the evidence was piling up (paw-prints in the milking sheds, tufts of red fur in the barbed wire, a tortured mewling lament filling the air at night) so much of it seemed so harmless compared to the genuine problems caused by the windmill breaking down. So harmless, in fact, that some animals began wondering whether the bad name foxes had on Manor Farm wasn't perhaps a little unfair. Or indeed whether, over the years since they had been banished, the species had grown somewhat less bloodthirsty. Even the starlings seemed split over how scared they should be. The mere mention of foxes sent some flanks into wild paroxysms of panic, while others barely batted a wing at the thought. In this way, as the weeks passed since the first sighting, the idea of a fox taking up residence on Manor Farm became less shocking than it had been for many a year.

Soon after, the animals of Manor Farm emerged from their stables and kennels and sheds and coops and nests into the cool sun of a January dawn, to be greeted with the vision of a sleek rust-coloured fox basking in the brilliant sunlight, grooming himself with long, luxurious passes of his rough tongue, unconcerned that he should be seen. Any horror the animals might have felt was tempered by a sense of familiarity and an odd lack of surprise; both brought on by the many hours they had spent discussing and debating just such a situation over the previous few weeks. Several of the cows and sheep approached the fox, some with fear – despite their size – others with curiosity, and most with a mix of the two. The fox stopped grooming himself and looked up. All the animals froze. The fox regarded them for an everlasting moment, and then his muzzle twisted into a heavily fanged, mischievous half-smile.

'Boo!' he said, an ironic twinkle in his eye. The half-smile broadened into a friendly grin. A huge wave of relief spread over the farmyard. A joke! And not any joke, but one which made light of their anxiety, which somehow had the effect of dispelling it. Even the hens had to wonder whether their fear had been a little misplaced.

'George,' the fox said, extending a limp paw, should one of the animals be brave enough to shake it. None of them were, despite the fact that he was so much smaller than many of the animals had imagined his kind to be. Most had expected something at least the size of a sheep, a cow even, with great, muscular flanks, sharp claws and thick fangs. George was sleek, not much bigger than Rocky, the farmyard moggy, and his pointed teeth were more-or-less hidden whenever his mouth was closed. His red pelt was spotless and he groomed it with an almost obsessive fussiness. He was also charming and, when some of the animals started expressing their concerns about his kind, answered with a disarming and sardonic wit.

'Is it true you hunt and eat rabbits?' one of the alpacas asked.

'Oh yes,' George drawled. 'I generally have two for lunch and two for dinner.' Then he winked at the rabbits huddled behind Marguerite's leg, and smiled at the others, baring his teeth, but not threateningly. Most of the animals understood this to mean he was heaping ridicule on the thought. Except the rabbits, who muttered among themselves that they would have felt better if he had denied it outright.

Having a fox around had a strange effect on Manor Farm. The species had been such a figure of fear for so long, that when actually faced with the genuine presence of one, many of the stories the animals had been told now seemed a little overripe. It was hard to believe that George was a fierce and ruthless hunter, an indiscriminate carnivore, when he went out of his way to be courteous to the rabbits, pigeons and hens. Or that he was deceitful and manipulative, and capable of bending other creatures to his will, when he was such an obliging and helpful presence around the farmyard. And while it was true that he possessed a caustic, cutting tongue, he certainly exhibited none of the malice and cruelty many of the animals had expected, and showed no sign of taking any pleasure from the wanton infliction of suffering.

Since so much of what the animals believed had recently turned out to be untrue, many of them decided that perhaps this new arrival should be given the benefit of the doubt. The dormice still kept their distance. In the privacy of their nest, they discussed how they could feel George's green eyes following them with a fierce intensity as they crossed the farmyard. They wanted to believe what all of the other animals seemed to; that the danger of the entire species had been overstated, or that this fox, in particular, was not like the others. Still, they could not ignore the instinct they felt throbbing from him. Neither could they ignore the lesson, which the other animals may have forgotten, but which had been passed down from one generation of dormice to the next: how last time there was a fox on the farm, he had led a concerted effort to eliminate their species not just from Manor Farm, but from the whole of England.

Perhaps surprisingly, for one of their natural predators, many of the geese got on particularly well with George. They appreciated his intelligence and wry outlook, and he could often be seen strolling across the farmyard or around the pool, deep in conversation with one or another of them. Haw-Haw was his biggest fan, but George sometimes looked a little embarrassed by his fawning attentions, and seemed more determined to befriend the more serious traditionalist geese. The ones who had not greeted his arrival with Haw-Haw's unalloyed enthusiasm, but who had not subjected him to a full-throated denunciation either.

After weeks of trips back and forth from the farmyard, and with Martha's encouraging her to keep on looking, Cassie had at last found the stretch of the quarry where newspapers and newsletters were dumped. Many of them had decomposed over the years, into a slurry of pulpy paper flakes that spilled across the surrounding rock like a sooty avalanche. But a significant number had been in some measure preserved from the elements by a jagged overhanging rock. Given how little interest most of the animals showed in the country, even the county, beyond Manor Farm, Cassie was astonished by the range of titles. There was the *Willingdon Courier*, the *Warbleton Echo*, the *Horam Harbinger*, the *Upper Dicker Ledger* and the *Lower Dicker Inquirer*. There was the *Crowborough Citizen*, the *Hellingley Herald* and the *Ringles Cross Advertiser*. There was the *Three Cups Corner Critic*, the *Dallington Democrat* and the *Polegate Pioneer*. There was even the *Pevensey Bay Planet*, a name Cassie had a certain difficulty weighing up.

The first ones she inspected were the more current editions, some from as recently as December, and while she wasn't interested in these, her thoughts turned to Martha. Might there be some mention of starlings on other farms in the region that she could pass on to her new friend? It wasn't long until she turned up an issue of the *Uckfield Outlook* that mentioned the starlings. It was a small article – given only a few inches beneath the lead story about a mysterious plague blighting several farms in Dorset, Wiltshire and Somerset – and told her little except that other farms had found themselves subject to similar visitations, but she dropped it into the wicker basket by her side. She had brought the basket all the way from the farm, in the hope that it would soon fill with newspapers pertinent to her undertaking. But for now it sat empty.

It wasn't until she had been poking around beneath the overhang for several days that Cassie finally found what she was looking for: *The Plough*. Hundreds and hundreds of issues beneath a mouldy tarpaulin.

The Council used to require the geese to typeset and print this newsletter on the old press in the farmhouse cellar, but the pigs had stopped it several years earlier, when it became clear few of the animals paid it any mind, preferring to get their news straight from their favourite goose's mouth. Cassie remembered *The Plough* from when she was a foal, how animals of every species pored over it with a fervour she had always admired. She remembered it being there. And she remembered it not being there. But she couldn't remember when the farm had passed from one state to the other.

Ever since uncovering the hundreds of issues of *The Plough*, Cassie had spent her visits working meticulously through them. First she tried to put them in order, based on how many '*Glorious Years since the Rebellion*' the masthead proclaimed. Then she set aside any newsletter that she thought might contain a clue, however small, or a hint, however slight, of the presence of her father on Manor Farm. So far, there had been slim pickings. Just two sheets, in fact. There was a photograph accompanying a story celebrating the First Choozin ('20 Glorious Years…'), in which a dark, equine figure lurked in the background stippling. There was also a newsletter ('Glorious Years' lost to rain damage) about the upgrading of the windmill. In the story, an animal in attendance said something that seemed to chime with the rare stories her mother had told her, when her sadness or drunkenness overcame the oath she had sworn never to talk about the one who'd abandoned her.

'Windmill or no windmill,' the unnamed animal was quoted as saying, 'life will go on as it always has.'

A week or so after George arrived, Haw-Haw called a special meeting in the Big Barn. The turnout was impressive. In the stalls alpacas, sheep and cows were pressed together, with Clive the Bullock occupying most of the front row. The hens and geckos nestled between the shoulders of these larger species, affording them some of the best views in the barn. In the rafters pigeons jostled for space with a few of the starlings who had left the flock to watch, while Balmoral had brought several of the roe deer family up from the orchard and seated them in the plush confines of the gallery. Most of the other geese were there too, as well as a few of the magpies, who had perched on the cash register and were cawing among themselves, feigning indifference while keeping one eye on the raised platform. Even the pigs had shown up, an indication of how seriously they took Haw-Haw's influence in the farmyard. Ribbons, Jumbo and Curly had set up picnic chairs to the side of the raised platform. Dermott, Pearl's zealous assistant, had cleared the cart of plush toys with his trotters, and the pair of them had settled down inside it like two giant novelty salt and pepper mills. Even Buttercup stood with Cosmo the owl near the fire exit, trying his best not to be seen.

Martha was surprised by the excitement in the room. Like a lot of the geese, she had been struggling to get any attention lately, as many of the animals now preferred to stay informed through the varied and gossipy chatter of the starlings, rather than what they saw as the geese's old-fashioned honking. And yet Haw-Haw, at least, was still able to draw a crowd. Perhaps because he was known to be a virtuoso performer, who'd developed his pantomime skills to a fine art, spluttering into an old loudhailer whenever he addressed the other animals, a gimmick which gave his soundings a party atmosphere.

By the time Haw-Haw appeared at the side of the raised platform, a little later than promised, the animals in the audience were champing with anticipation. Life on Manor Farm hadn't been much fun of late, and they were keen for Haw-Haw to distract them with a scandal.

From Martha's spot in the stalls she had been able to listen in as the animals shared their thoughts about what, exactly, Haw-Haw might have to say. Most of it was rather banal. Rumours put about by the starlings with little evidence to back them up:

'It's going to be some scandal involving the cost of insulating the vivarium,' one hen suggested.

'More likely about how Buttercup plans to downgrade our fodder,' suggested a sheep.

'I heard he's discovered yet another outrageous way the WUF wastes *our* money!' cooed one of the pigeons. It was the usual farmyard worries and gossip. Martha had heard all the stories before

'Look, he's starting!' bleated one of the alpacas. Martha turned back to the raised platform. Haw-Haw had waddled out, feathers proudly fluffed, and was waiting for the crowd to hush. Satisfied, he brought the loudhailer to his beak.

'Some material,' he honked, 'has come into my possession that will surely have a decisive impact on the Choozin next year.'

Those who had spotted Buttercup turned to observe his reaction. If the First Beast was concerned, he disguised it well, looking more amused than unsettled. Haw-Haw now indicated the low stool beside him, upon which sat a portable cassette player. He positioned the loudhailer in front of it, and pressed down one of the buttons with his wingtip. The voice that dribbled out of the small speaker was faint, but undeniably Buttercup's:

'...I made a lot of money when the windmill stopped...' it crackled. '...I'd have been a fool not to...' The animals in the audience looked around at each other for confirmation of what they were hearing. Haw-Haw rested his wing on the pause button, giving them the time they needed for it to sink in. When he was satisfied, he lifted his wing and the tape continued:

'It's all in the WUF, of course... I'd never be mad enough to keep it on Manor Farm... Most of the animals here... are too stupid to understand... I'd give us five years before the whole farm is sold off, stripped for scrap by Foxwood and Pinchfield...'

The tape had finished now and the animals had turned to look at Buttercup, waiting for him to speak. Mustering all of the assurance that more than five years as First Beast had given him, he strode across the floor of the Big Barn and took to the stage. Haw-Haw nodded his welcome and offered Buttercup the loudhailer, but Buttercup waved it off. The look on his face was one of pure bemusement at the vulgarity and obviousness of the prank.

'Listen,' he said to the crowd. 'I think you all know I'm a pretty honest sort of pig.' The animals again looked to each other, unsure what to think.

'Were you honest with us about the redecoration of the farmhouse?' Jumbo hollered from beside the raised platform. Buttercup snorted with derision. The other animals knew that snort only too well; many of them used to enjoy it when they were on his side. Now, it sounded condescending. Ribbons was also glaring at Jumbo, who had otherwise been uncharacteristically well-behaved and discrete since the pear-bobbing catastrophe. Last year's lavish redecoration of the farmhouse bedrooms, paid for by farm money, had been a scandal that reflected equally badly on all the pigs, not just Buttercup. While the pigs on the Council may have thought the story was old and uninteresting, many of the animals were nodding now.

'We apologised for that and paid back the money,' he said. 'And besides, I think there are more import…'

'And were you honest about the failure of your little adventure to Percy Cox's, about the state in which you left things, about how much it cost Manor Farm? About the *real* reasons for the intervention?'

Buttercup looked at Haw-Haw with wide-eyed surprise.

'You and the other geese were the ones who *encouraged* me to…'

'And what about the windmill?' Haw-Haw honked, drowning out Buttercup. 'Were you honest with us about that?' This last question animated the animals. Few of them had drawn a line from the scandal about redecorating the farmhouse, to the intervention at Percy Cox's, to the windmill. But with Haw-Haw's guidance they could now see that there was indeed a connection: In each of these events Buttercup had played them, the Manor Beasts, for fools.

'Look,' Buttercup said, his voice catching. 'We always made our decisions based on the best information we had at the time. Trust me…'

'*Trust* you?' Haw-Haw honked with exaggerated disbelief. The gathered animals bayed and cawed and bleated. Haw-Haw craned his long neck up to Buttercup's ear, his beak almost clipping the pig's skin. 'It seems to me,' he said beneath the hubbub, 'that you have given them precious little reason to *trust you.*'

'You changed my words,' Buttercup hissed. 'I demand you play the original tapes.'

'What original tapes?' Haw-Haw said, scuffing the boards with his heel. 'And besides, it would make no difference. Perhaps you should ask yourself why that is.' Buttercup turned away from Haw-Haw and faced the animals again. To Martha it looked like he was straining to hide his panic.

'My fellow animals,' he bellowed. 'These tapes are fakes!'

Haw-Haw once again lifted his loudhailer to his beak: 'My friends,' he cried. 'He thinks you're too stupid to understand what you've heard with your own ears.'

At this the animals let loose, filling the Big Barn with a terrible racket. Buttercup, shaken, turned on his trotters. Descending from the platform, he hurried out of the room, a rancid tomato just missing his head and exploding on the door jamb.

The First Beast resigned that very night. In the letter he left on his desk, Buttercup once again denied Haw-Haw's charges and warned the animals that they were being led along a dangerous path, from which it would be difficult to return. He also added that he knew that regaining trust was an uphill labour for which he no longer had the fodder in his belly. A few hours later he was spotted by several of the starlings standing on his four trotters at the farm's gate, wearing a ski jacket and with a suitcase at his feet. He looked tired, the starlings reported, but also oddly relieved, as if an enormous burden had been lifted from him. After he had been waiting for a few minutes, a taxi cab pulled up and the human driver helped him load his cases into the boot. As Buttercup climbed into the taxi, he was seen to mouth something back at the farm which some of the watching starlings lip-read as 'good luck' but which others were sure was 'good riddance'.

Cassie had come to the drinking pool, she said, to give Martha something she'd found at the quarry. It was a newspaper called the *Uckfield Outlook*. At first Martha didn't understand why the mule had brought it. What interest, really, was some pestilence in a distant county when things were falling apart under her beak? Cassie sensed her scepticism.

'The starlings,' Cassie said, nosing the small article at the bottom of the page. Of course, the starlings. Buttercup's resignation had rather pushed them from the young goose's mind. She read it quickly, determined there was little new, and tucked it away in her nest, under a thick patch of moss and lichen.

'Thank you,' she said. But it was clear Cassie had something else she wanted to ask.

'I thought there had to be a Choozin,' Cassie said. 'To select the First Beast. Now that Buttercup's gone.' Martha too had thought there would be a Choozin, but quickly learned that the Farm Charter thought differently.

'Choozins can only take place on the day of the summer solstice,' Martha said. 'It's the Council of Animals who select the First Beast until then... and the Council chose Ribbons.'

'But why?' Cassie asked, frowning hard. 'Ribbons is the leader of the Jonesists. I thought the Animalists controlled the Council.'

'They do,' Martha said. 'Or at least they did. But not by much. Not by enough, it turned out.'

Martha thought back to the special Council meeting she'd attended in the dining room of the farmhouse on the morning of the previous day. Two candidates for First Beast had come forward: Ribbons for the Jonesists and Cosmo the owl for the

Animalists. Cosmo had an excellent record from his time as Buttercup's Quartermaster, his organisation of the pear-and-apple (apple-and-pear) harvest the previous autumn had impressed pigs from both droves. But as the first wild animal, indeed the first non-pig, to stand for First Beast, his candidacy had been greeted with derision from the Jonesists and a certain bafflement from his own side.

And now that Buttercup had gone, the vote was on a scythe-edge. The Animalists had twelve affiliated pigs, and the Jonesists had ten. There was also the one unaffiliated member: Quaver, a timid, jaundiced teacup pig, who always resolutely refused to take sides. He was known to sit, ignored, at the foot of the dining-room table, muttering under his breath – when challenged – that 'surely both droves have something to offer'.

Still, Martha had been confident that Cosmo would squeak it. Even if Quaver tipped Ribbons's way, there remained twelve Animalist pigs, and surely they would all vote for the owl.

'But Ribbons still won?' Cassie said.

'Eleven votes to ten,' Martha said. Cassie frowned even harder.

'That's only twenty-one votes,' she said after a moment. Martha nodded.

'Pearl and Dermott didn't show up,' she said. 'They sent a little porker in with a message that they couldn't countenance supporting a candidate who betrayed the dream of True Animalism by refusing to even acknowledge the existence of Sugarcandy Mountain.' Cassie's frown was replaced with distilled confusion.

'Sugarcandy *what?*'

'Don't ask,' Martha said. 'Some old farmyard legend, apparently.'

'So they handed the position of First Beast to Ribbons,' Cassie said.

'At least until the Choozin in June, yes,' Martha said.

'I never knew the rules were so very odd,' Cassie said. 'And I'm not that young.'

Martha thought then of the first time she'd met Duke, when he'd shown her how a spider's web hangs together in such perfect harmony… until the moment it doesn't.

The two animals stood in silence. Cassie's heavy belly rising and falling with her breath, inches from Martha's head. A belly supported by ribs that were longer and thicker, by many orders of magnitude, than any of Martha's slender bones. At that moment, the goose was almost overcome by the extent of their physical distinctness. And yet here they were: friends, of a fashion. And there were all the animals of the farm too, from mule, to goose, to pig, to cow, to dormouse, to magpie, to gecko, to pigeon, to hen, to rabbit, to alpaca – and, yes – to the starlings as well. All so different and yet somehow, with a little effort on all of their parts, able to live alongside each other in something resembling harmony. At least they had been. She thought of Duke's spider's web again.

'Do you think it will be alright?' Cassie asked after a while. 'With Ribbons, I mean.'

It wasn't the first time Martha had heard that question. The previous day she'd heard it uttered across the estate, from the farmhouse dining table, to the Big Barn, to the hayfield and the drinking pool. Whatever the animals thought of Buttercup, she was surprised to realise that they feared the end of his rule. She did too. He could be arrogant, condescending and, they had recently discovered, profoundly dishonest. But he'd also projected a calmness and competence that many of them found reassuring.

And yet, when Ribbons had taken to the stage in the Big Barn to deliver his first speech as First Beast to a somewhat meagre crowd of animals, and promised – in a voice that sounded like a deliberate imitation of his predecessor – to do things that sounded oddly similar to what Buttercup had already been doing, a murmur of reassurance had passed over the room.

Similar things, but not the same, Martha noticed. Whereas Buttercup had promised the chicken coop would be repainted each year, Ribbons assured the animals only that it would be kept in 'excellent condition'. Likewise, while Buttercup had committed to the vivarium's temperature never dropping below thirty-eight degrees, Ribbons instead promised that it would always be kept 'sufficiently warm'. He had also sacked Cosmo as Quartermaster and appointed Curly, the Baston pig who had previously challenged him for the leadership of the Jonesists, in the owl's stead.

These differences all concerned Martha, but had seemed to matter less to the animals in the Big Barn that evening. Indeed, as Martha listened in to their conversations once Ribbons had left the stage, she heard several animals confess that, in those first minutes of Ribbons's tenure at least, had Buttercup been standing beside his ersatz successor, they would have had some difficulty saying which pig was which.

Cassie stood, waiting for an answer. But what answer could Martha really give? *Would* it be alright?

'I just don't know,' she said.

FEBRUARY

One evening in late winter Martha noticed that the water along Duke's side of the drinking pool had turned an extraordinarily vivid green. She decided to make her way around to have a closer look. When she arrived, the first thing she noticed was that two other lines had been drawn in the mud beside the first.

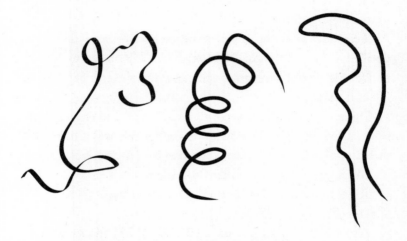

Martha thought back to how the two greylags had mocked her for even wondering if there might be some meaning there, and felt a little sick with the echo of the shame. And yet not only were there two new squiggles on the mud, but Duke must have done everything he could to preserve the first one from the elements these last two months.

'Word is that they've let a fox back on the farm,' Duke said before she could greet him. He was looking out across the pool. The light from the setting sun passing through his sunglasses cast a dark green veil over his face.

'George,' Martha said. 'He seems harmless.'

Duke sighed. 'Would never've happened if they hadn't done for old Benjamin like they did,' he said, shaking his head.

'Who?' Martha asked.

'Old Benjamin *remembered*,' Duke said. 'Which is exactly why they did for him.'

'Who's Benjamin?' Martha tried again. But Duke only rolled his eyes, then turned back to the pool. Now, his gaze seemed not to be trained on the water, but on the grassy knoll and the unmoving windmill.

'I can hear him now: If we let the fox back on, and the fox just does what foxes do, is that the fox's fault?' He turned to Martha and let his aviator sunglasses slide down to the end of his beak. 'Or is it ours?'

Duke, as usual, didn't seem to be in a mood to explain himself, and Martha was by now quite used to his ways. Instead of questioning him further, she pointed to the patch of green water.

'What do you make of that?' she asked.

'Algae,' he said. 'Deadly poisonous. And hard to control, if left unchecked.'

'At least it's only this one small patch,' Martha said. Duke pulled hard on his cigarette.

'That's not how this works,' he said, looking over his sunglasses and into Martha's eyes.

'What do you mean?'

'The advance of algae, like with all bad, bad things, is existential...' Duke paused, checked himself. '*Exp*onential. Slow at first, then sudden. Nowhere, then everywhere. There's a tipping point, and I'm afraid to say our pool is already past it.'

Duke was right. When Martha next looked at the drinking pool the following morning, the entire surface was green.

Cassie was exhausted. She had been coming to the quarry for almost five months – from autumn, through winter, and now, as the first whiff of spring reached her wide, leathery nostrils. And so far she had found nothing new about her father. No clear confirmation that he had ever existed at all. Had she been stupid to believe her mother's claims that he had meant something, that he had somehow been important in the farm's story? Pigs were important. Dogs too. And sometimes even horses. But… She snorted at her own stupidity. And yet she also knew that she wouldn't stop coming, wouldn't stop looking. That stopping would somehow hurt more than keeping going and finding nothing.

'I will look harder,' she muttered unthinkingly, then smiled. That was her cart horse ancestry speaking. The ancestry that condemned her to continue this thankless search. A search which had taken its toll on her body too. She had lost count of how many shards of glass she'd removed from her hooves, and had almost stopped noticing the prickly rash on her flanks, caused, she thought, by whatever had been in the rusted aerosol can that had exploded over her several weeks earlier. Still, she hoped and hoped, beyond all hope, for a sign that she wasn't wrong to carry on looking. And later that day she found one.

Beneath a pile of plastic bin bags lay an old leather suitcase, warped and patinated with age, its clasp rusted shut. Cassie had found and opened many similar cases these past months. Most had been empty. Some were full of old moth-eaten clothes. Inside one she had disturbed a whole family of wild rats, who'd hissed and snapped at her as she'd begged their forgiveness for upsetting their home.

She nudged this new case with her muzzle. It didn't move. Not an inch. Whatever was inside was heavy. She tore off the clasp with a flick of her teeth, and flipped the lid open. Inside were several dozen books, their spines warped, their pages spotted with age. Most appeared to be human romance stories, or tales of war, but one caught her eye. Its cover was divided into two triangles, one grey and one green, that somehow reminded her of the farm's windmill. And yet as she examined it, a feeling of astonishment rose up within her. If the text on the cover was to be believed, this book told the very story she had been looking for all these months. Or part of it, anyway.

She looked for reasons not to trust it. It was written by a human, that was grounds enough to toss it away unread. It also claimed to be a story about fairies, but even the sheep weren't stupid enough to believe they existed. The white lettering on the cover slanted in a way that she found oddly suspicious. But who was she trying to fool? Cassie licked her lips, and settled her croup down onto an old patchwork cushion. Dark storm clouds were gathering overhead, and all warmth had fled the air, but she didn't notice. She dipped her head, and turned the hard cover over with her tongue. She flipped past the sheets of front matter. In such haste was she to read the story, she didn't even pause to notice the plate glued to the first leaf.

This book belongs to
NAꟼO⅃ꓘON

This book, by the human with the name of a river, told the story of Manor Farm at the time of the Great Rebellion. There were parts that were familiar to Cassie, and others that were entirely new. She had always thought a straight line could be traced from the

Rebellion, to the founding of the droves and the First Choozin, and to the prosperous, free, if troubled, Manor Farm they all knew today. But if this book was to be believed that was not the case at all. The animals' freedom had been fought for, bloodily. Then betrayed. Then lost. Nothing was a given.

There were words scrawled in many of the margins. Words like 'LIAR!!', 'WRONG!', and 'CROOKED BORE-WELL'. But Cassie read through these, paid them no mind, ignored them for the puff and bluster of the crazed ego that they so clearly were. And why? Because there *he* was. Not on every page, but on many of them. Not the most heroic of the beasts in the tale, but certainly the most enduring. Perhaps the most insightful. Possibly even the most noble... at least Cassie thought so.

Windmill or no windmill, he said, life would go on as it had always gone on – that is, badly.

Cassie nodded.

Things never had been, nor ever could be much better or much worse – hunger, hardship and disappointment being, so he said, the unalterable law of life.

Cassie sighed.

He would say that God had given him a tail to keep the flies off, but that he would sooner have had no tail and no flies.

Cassie smiled.

As she read, and despite the tragedy of the tale, she felt a lightness of spirit overcome her, as if the bridle around her heart had been loosened several notches. There was his species, in black and white: donkey. And there was his name too. The first time she'd seen this long, peculiar word she'd read it twice, three times, to be sure she wasn't dreaming. She wasn't. She spoke it out loud to herself, trying out its sound in her mouth.

'Benjamin,' she said. 'Benjamin.'

Since the arrival of the first breeding pair of alpacas, several generations earlier, their troughs had been filled with the same chewy green balls of Pilkington's Organic Fodder that the sheep ate. One day, however, as the spring equinox approached, the alpacas noticed that their troughs contained crunchy grey cartridges. The taste and texture of this new fodder left the alpacas in little doubt that it was a lower-grade replacement.

The alpacas were curious to know why they had to suffer this new fodder while the sheep continued to dine on Pilkington's, and petitioned Curly for answers. Ribbons's appointment of Curly as Manor Farm's Quartermaster had been hailed by the geese as an ingenious way for the new First Beast to neutralise his erstwhile rival. For Quartermaster was a thankless job. Over the years, the animals of Manor Farm had come to consider being well-fed their birthright. They therefore felt no obligation of gratitude to the beast that ensured the farm's supplies. If there was a problem, on the other hand, it was the Quartermaster who was blamed. Curly appeared on the porch at once, almost as if he had been waiting for their challenge.

'It was brought to the Council's attention,' he whined, 'that each alpaca consumes twice as much fodder as each sheep. Fairness requires, in these straightened times, that the money spent on fodder be the same for each individual animal. Since portions cannot be halved without starving your kind, a *high*-quality replacement fodder was found. But let me reassure you, that this new fodder necessarily meets the stringent quality controls imposed on us by the WUF.' Some of the alpacas seemed to accept Curly's argument, others looked less convinced.

'But our wool sells for three times as much as the sheep's,' piped up one of the flock's younger males. 'Surely we pay our way.'

'You most certainly do, my dear camelid,' Curly replied, with the scrupulous politeness for which he was known. 'But you must see that it would be *terribly* unfair to discriminate on those grounds when the price of wool is something over which your poor brother sheep have no control.' Before the alpacas had time to consult on this, Curly dipped his head, narrowed his eyes, and spoke again: 'I also hesitate to remind you that this change would not have been necessary had your *adored* Buttercup not almost bankrupted Manor Farm.' Several of the alpacas later confessed that a chill had passed along their spines when they heard this. 'Still,' Curly added. 'Should you wish to pursue the matter, I would *happily* organise a consultation with all concerned animals.'

'But there are five times as many sheep as us,' bleated the same young alpaca.

'Five times?' Curly said, with a thin smile. 'That is unfortunate.'

The young alpaca had one more question: 'Have similar savings been made on the pigs' fodder?'

'That is a *very* interesting point,' Curly said. 'For which I do not have the answer at my trotter-tips. But rest assured, I will make *every* endeavour to investigate, and keep you abreast of whatever I can snuffle out.' He turned and strutted into the farmhouse.

It took Curly an entire week to respond further and, when he did, it was in a very convoluted pronouncement, read by a more junior pig. In order to maintain the correct functioning of their brains, Curly wrote, it was necessary for the pigs to eat a highly varied and nutritionally rich diet. Nevertheless, the pronouncement went on, Curly would speak to their supplier (a merchant with a name unfamiliar to the alpacas but which sounded something like *Fortnumunmason*) about where any savings could be made.

One of Ribbons's first actions after succeeding Buttercup was to order the removal of the graffiti from the day of the Whopping Commotion. A scaffold was erected in front of the Big Barn's east window, and a huge tarpaulin hung from it to obscure the work from view. As none of the animals on Manor Farm were particularly suited to paint removal, Ribbons contracted a team of Pinchfield pelicans to complete the work, a decision that caused the alpacas to ask, as they crunched on their dusty new fodder, where the funds for that had come from.

After several weeks, the work was complete, and Ribbons gathered a small group of Jonesist supporters (cows, deer, certain sheep and several pigs) to witness the unveiling of the restored window. Cassie, who was making her way across the farmyard, stopped to watch from the back of the crowd. When Ribbons tugged a cord and the tarpaulin fell, the gathered animals erupted in applause at the sight of the farm's revered motto once again shimmering on the glass for all to see. It read: MANOR FARM FOR MANOR BEASTS.

Only Cassie didn't bray her applause. Her memory wasn't flawless, but it was better than most, and she knew those weren't the words that had been obscured all those months. Words which themselves were different from those she had read in that book. Clive the Bullock was standing beside her, half a dozen chirping starlings lined up along his back. He was admiring the work.

'Are you sure that's right?' Cassie asked him. Clive looked at her with barely concealed spite.

'It's what's engraved on the glass, ass,' he said, managing both to insult Cassie, and not quite answer her question.

Later that same morning, Dunning and Kruger were spotted by some of the pigeons. It was the first time the bull terriers had been seen on Manor Farm since the Whopping Commotion, when they had fled with the man from Whymper. The birds had watched the dogs remove the boards and padlock from the kennels and go in. Within minutes, the lights had been turned on, and the familiar symphony of telephones ringing and fax machines whinnying could be heard drifting from the windows. The dogs then left the kennels, pulling behind them a cart loaded with what looked like metal braces, big enough for a horse or cow, as well as several large, glass syringes. They dragged the cart up the grassy knoll, unloaded its contents into the dynamo room, then went inside and closed the door behind them. That afternoon the windmill's vanes finally started turning again, and much faster than before. All signs pointed to the dogs, and the electricity market, being back in business.

As news of the dogs' return spread across the farm, an anger rose from the orchard to the ploughland, to the spinney. A spontaneous congregation formed, of animals from almost all of Manor Farm's species. With no one animal leading the way, the group made its way to the farmhouse to demand an explanation from Ribbons. The new First Beast granted them an audience and nodded slowly as they expressed their concern that the dogs would once again wreak havoc on Manor Farm's coffers.

'While it is true that the demand for electricity collapsed, surely you all remember that it was Buttercup's wastefulness that strangled the market,' said Ribbons after they had finished. Many of the animals squinted as they struggled to square this pronouncement with their memories. Ribbons went on: 'Indeed, had the dogs only had freer rein, many of the problems Manor Farm now faces could have been avoided. So gifted are Dunning and Kruger with money matters, in fact, that you'll be delighted to learn that I have, this very day, also given them responsibility for selling the farm's eggs, wool and milk. For after all, as the third verse of "Beasts of England" reminds us…' And he sang:

> 'Rings shall vanish from our noses
> Cruel whips no more shall crack
> Free to pursue our endeavours
> Free from rules holding us back!'

The animals looked at each other doubtfully. The lines about rings and cruel whips certainly sounded familiar, and they remembered the hymn being full of exhortations to grasp freedom, but… there was something wrong about the version Ribbons had just sung. Unfortunately, none of them had checked the words to 'Beasts of England' of late. Some of the older animals in the congregation, like Marguerite the Holstein, had vague memories of there once being a creature on the farm whose duty it was to keep track of such things. Not just the words to 'Beasts of England', but all of the stories from Manor Farm's past. But it had been so long since they had seen this animal that they had precisely no recollection of its name or species. Ribbons's explanation left the group divided. Most of the cows accepted it. They had long thought Buttercup had frittered too much money on the lower animals, so it didn't require much for them to accept that this very wastefulness was what had almost brought the farm to its knees. On the other hand, the hens and pigeons, the happy beneficiaries of much of this 'wasted' money, were left unconvinced and even angrier than before.

The sheep and the alpacas were divided almost entirely along species lines, as they so often were these days. The alpacas had lost all faith in Ribbons since their fodder had been changed, and had started to remember Buttercup with a certain fondness. While the sheep had never understood Buttercup's explanation of the farm's woes, they found there to be an attractive simplicity to the way Ribbons presented things, which made him easier to believe. And so the congregation split. Those animals that decided to believe Ribbons, at least for now, dispersed to their sties and stables and paddocks. Those that didn't turned away from the farmhouse and started making their way towards the kennels, a destructive fire in their bellies.

The kennels were only a short walk across the farmyard, and yet in the time it took for the animals to reach them, their group had grown again. Those they had lost to Ribbons's slick-tongue were replaced twofold, by rabbits and rats, two species so downtrodden that neither drove ever addressed them, as well as by a colourful array of animals from the farmyard Set, those modern young beasts who'd rejected traditional animal life in favour of roles serving the human visitors to the farm. When the group reached the kennels, they realised that the pigeons had not told them everything. For they saw that a new fence had been erected around the buildings. There was also a sign: black lettering on a yellow background read 'CAUTION: ELECTRIC FENCE', accompanied by a diagram of a black sheep being struck by four bolts of lightning. The marchers stopped dead. Frustrated by this new obstacle, feeling beaten and helpless and as if they had nowhere left to turn, the fighting spirit began to drain from them.

One of the rabbits shrieked. Above them a vast flank of starlings was gathering. At first there seemed to be no logic to its movements, a churning mass of feathers darting in every direction across a patch of sky. Then, slowly, they began coalescing, turning spirals around an invisible column before, without warning, shooting high into the sky, in tight formation, like an arrow shot from a bow. When it had reached several hundred feet above the farmyard, this arrow of starlings turned and plunged down towards the kennels. The roof stood no chance. Amid a splintering of wood and a shattering of glass the starlings disappeared into the kennels and then, moments later, Dunning and Kruger, burst through the doors, barking and snapping as the starlings pursued them into the farmyard. The animals watched in wonder as the starlings toyed with the dogs, chasing them this way and that in a perverted parody of the way humans had once used dogs to herd sheep.

'Ungrateful undomesticates!' Dunning (or was it Kruger?) snarled at the cheering mob of animals. 'After all we did for you!'

'You were oh-so-happy to live in ignorance when times were good!' Kruger (or Dunning?) joined. 'You dirty, stupid beasts!'

After several minutes of this back-and-forth the starlings changed tack. They harried the dogs out of the farmyard and towards the drinking pool, swooping and diving and harassing them into its lurid green shallows.

The marchers were exuberant. Even those who had lived in fear of the starlings since their arrival allowed themselves to wonder whether a new day had come to Manor Farm, an era in which the pigs and dogs could be held to account not only by other pigs and dogs, but by the coordinated effort of hundreds of the farm's tiniest and seemingly most insignificant creatures.

The following day, several strange things happened. Dermott, Pearl's second in command, took to a pear-crate just after sunrise to praise the heroic actions of 'our dear leader', in leading the glorious, thousand-animal march on the kennels. This caused a certain confusion among the animals, most of whom didn't remember seeing either Pearl or Dermott the previous day. But then, they had to admit that things had happened so quickly, and so chaotically, that it wasn't impossible that Dermott was telling the truth.

The morning also saw a visit to the farm by a sturdy nanny goat, wearing WUF insignia and petitioning for an urgent audience with Ribbons. Membership of the Wealden Union gave most animals free passage from one farm in the association to another. However, tradition dictated that officials, from other farms or the WUF itself, should not enter any of the farms in the union without first being given permission. Ribbons ignored the petition, and after waiting for several hours, the nanny goat departed a little before lunchtime.

Then, in the afternoon, the starlings reported that a vast electrified net had been installed above both the kennels and the farmhouse, clearly intended to see off any future attack from the sky. The kennels themselves had not only been fully repaired but the surrounding fence had been extended to take in the knoll and the windmill, from which a new thick black cable now extended, running down the knoll, across the ploughland and the orchard, and off in the direction of Pinchfield Farm. Activity at the kennels also picked up again, almost as if nothing had happened the previous day. Indeed, the dogs were so busy, and so cocky in the way they went about their business, that some of the animals started wondering how much of a difference the showy actions of the starlings the previous day had really made at all.

MARCH

W hen the crocuses were coming into bloom, word reached the farmyard that a number of lean-tos had been spotted among the refuse in the quarry. Most of the geese had long grown too impassive to waddle much beyond the paddock – why bother, when the animals only wanted to listen to the starlings – but this didn't stop them going to extravagant lengths to imagine the state of things out beyond the far field. Haw-Haw in particular, whose version involved packs of slavering carnivorous beasts, come to Manor Farm determined to upset the genteel balance of life there. And since Haw-Haw had recently got hold of a battery-powered megaphone, his version was currently the most heard across the estate.

So much so, that Balmoral the roe deer once again started demanding a moat be dug around the farm, and for the gate to be secured with a padlock. Otherwise, how could they possibly tell if an animal was on the farm by rights or if they were a stray? Ribbons expressed sympathy for the idea but was disappointed to tell Balmoral that the right to roam agreed by the Wealden Union of Farmers explicitly forbade moats and fences. He also added that it was his experience that most animals preferred to live and grow old where they were born and raised, and only those who felt they really had to move did.

When the old stag's complaints started to find supporters among animals of different species, Ribbons had the pelicans paint two columns on the east window of the Big Barn, just beneath the farm's motto. The left column was headed ᛘᗅᴎOR BᴈᴀᏄTS and the right ᴎOT ᛘᗅᴎOR BᴈᴀᏄTS. In the columns themselves he had the seabirds paint the words 'ᗅᴎiᛖᗅLS bORNᴇᒷ ON ᛖᗅᴎOᴙ ᖸᗅᴙᛖ' to the left, and to the right 'hᴜᛖᗅNS' and 'Stᴙᗅy ᗅᴎiᛖᗅLS'.

That way, at least any stray animal that made its way onto the farm would know the lay of the land. Although most of the animals saw nothing objectionable in the distinction, a few of them did pause to wonder why the line separating the columns had been extended all the way down to the ground. It also left the Pinchfield pelicans, who were neither born on Manor Farm nor stray, unsure in which column their kind would be placed.

assie hadn't been to the quarry for several weeks. Spring meant visitors, and visitors meant mule rides. It also meant a steady tramp of noisy human children and their harassed parents dropping their ice creams and candy floss, screaming at the animals (and each other) for no reason Cassie could fathom, and trying to finger her muzzle with their sticky little digits.

But as soon as Monday came around, and the farm was closed, she trotted in the direction of the quarry with a haste born of indignation, itself born of a feeling of ownership over the piles of scrap and refuse that she hadn't realised she felt until she'd heard about the arrival of the strays.

The overhaul was extraordinary. It wasn't just two or three lean-tos, but a whole labyrinth of them, built, often ingeniously, from sections of fence, corrugated iron and drystack that had been dumped there over the years. Cassie counted close to fifty animals: pigs, goats, cows and horses, as well as other creatures that she had only read about in *Animals of the World*, a colourful old picture book she'd scoured, on this very spot, several months earlier. She identified a family of capybaras, a gang of male ostriches, and a wallaby with several of her emaciated young asleep in her pouch. It was obvious that all of these animals had suffered in one way or another on their long journeys to the quarry.

Cassie wondered what the new residents were doing there. Where had they come from and why? She also wondered if she would frighten them, or if they would act with aggression towards her. In fact they seemed grateful that their presence had finally been acknowledged, and were keen to share their stories. Some of them, she discovered, were wild by birth, and had come to escape the nasty, brutish and short existence nature reserved for them.

Others had suffered at the hands of humans, both as working beasts or as 'pets', a word Cassie had only ever heard used as an insult. As she spoke to animal after animal, Cassie was distressed to learn that much of England beyond the boundaries of the WUF was in a more parlous state than she'd ever realised, and that a lot of animals had been displaced and were moving from county to county, farm to farm, desperately looking for a place to settle. And since Manor Farm was the first estate to throw off the bondage of servitude to humans, many of them assumed the welcome there would be warmer than on some of the other farms in Wealden.

One conversation with a young sow startled Cassie. The flesh of the pig's ear was torn, as if a ring had been ripped from it, and she spoke with a thick Norfolk accent. She was a Shore Farm pig who had fled her home to escape the horrible treatment meted out there. Cassie was almost overcome with delight at the good news she could share.

'But haven't you heard?' she said. 'Percy Cox is gone. Buttercup saw to that.'

While much of Buttercup's legacy had been tarnished since he'd quit, most of the animals on Manor Farm remained proud of the sacrifices they had made, several years earlier, to secure the freedom of Shore Farm's inhabitants from the tyrant Percy Cox. Which was why Cassie was taken aback when the sow snorted.

'It's not Percy Cox I'm fleeing,' she said. While it was true that Buttercup had helped evict the barbarous old farmer and install a Council of Animals, the sow explained that this had quickly collapsed after Manor Farm's support ran out. Before any of them knew it, a skulk of greyhound foxes had descended from a nearby wood and taken control of the farm, which they now ruled with a bloody claw. For many of the animals, life on Shore

Farm was now as bad as, or even worse than, it had been under Percy Cox. He was at least predictable, whereas the foxes were cruel and mercurial. Buttercup and Manor Farm had abandoned her, the sow said, which was why she had made the journey here.

As dusk began to fall over the quarry, Cassie noticed a small shelter that appeared to be built from some of the very books she had found in the previous few months. She poked her head inside, almost bumping noses with a young horse, the skinniest example of his kind Cassie had ever seen. He told her that he had been bred and raised to work in Simmonds & Son's MBM factory. There was something familiar about that name, but Cassie couldn't say exactly what. She asked what MBM was, and the horse told her that it stood for 'meat and bone meal', a substance rendered from the carcasses of animals and used as cheap fuel. His job, he explained, had been to drag cartloads of dead cows, sheep, pigs and even horses ('My own kin!') from the factory courtyard to the conveyor belts that fed the vast rendering vats. The humans that managed the factory threatened the animals enslaved there with a trip to the vat should they refuse to work or request better conditions. So when, one evening, the drunk night watchman had forgotten to lock the door to their stable, several of them had escaped. The horse was the only one to make it this far.

'Manor Farm has many problems,' Cassie said, her voice quivering with emotion. 'But we would never treat fellow beasts like that.'

'So I thought,' said the horse. 'Which was why I came here. But when I was building my stable, I found this.' He passed Cassie a ledger book. Inked on the cover were the words:

Manor Farm: Livestock Valu of Animals

135

Cassie dropped the book to the ground and nudged it open with her nose. Each page was separated, left to right, into three columns: ᴀⱨimaL, NU∧B∃R, and maᴙKt vaLᴜ. Cassie read the list with a mounting feeling of disgust: *Sheep, Cows, Hens, Horses...* Every season of every year since the Great Rebellion, every species of animal was subjected to this monstrous calculation. Except for the pigs. And the dogs of course! In fact their paw prints were, quite literally, all over every page of this book. As she read, a thought occurred to her. She skimmed on down the list: *Alpacas, Pigeons, Rabbits...* There! There it was! Right at the bottom. And not just on the first page, but on every page for the first twenty-five years since the rebellion. Animal: Donkey. Number: 1. And in the Market Value column a price which fluctuated with the years, but which was always accompanied by the word, 'knacker'.

Then, in the autumn of the twenty-fifth year, that line vanished. And it never came back.

That evening Martha spotted Cassie tramping back past the drinking pool, lost in her thoughts. She beat her wings to catch the mule's attention. Then, when Cassie looked up she honked: 'I've got a whole bag of broken biscuits that one of the humans dropped... if you fancy sharing?' Cassie smiled, and Martha understood that she was happy for a conversation, biscuits or not.

Cassie looked across the reed beds towards the pool, which glowed a phosphorescent green, despite the twilight. There was not a single inch of its surface that hadn't been colonised by the toxic algae, and bodies of dead fish pocked the shore.

'Makes you wonder why they come,' she said.

'Who?' Martha asked. Cassie told her about the strays, about the poor horse that had escaped from the MBM factory in Somerset. Martha felt the compass in her head shudder, although she wasn't sure why.

'Not much point asking if that's good to drink, I suppose,' Cassie said, nodding at the water. Martha shook her head. 'Only I'm getting a little sick of the metallic taste of the well water.'

'Metallic?' Martha asked.

'Ever since the humans came back, they won't stop throwing coins down there,' Cassie said. 'And of course the Council won't do anything about it because...'

'The visitors bring home the bacon,' Martha said. Cassie smiled.

'Don't let the pigs hear you speaking like that,' she said.

'You'd think they'd worry less about the visitors,' Martha went on. 'Now that the dogs are back, I mean.'

Cassie started. The news seemed to have surprised her. Angered her, even.

'Dunning and Kruger?' she said. 'When?'

'Last month,' Martha said. 'At least the starlings gave them quite a hard time.' Cassie lifted her head and looked at the windmill. Martha followed her gaze. The sails, despite the still air, was turning at quite a clip. 'Not that it made much difference,' Martha added.

A strange look came over Cassie's face then. Somewhere between resignation, realisation and relief.

'Windmill or no windmill,' the mule said. 'Life will go on as it has always gone on.'

It was true that the windmill's sails were once again whizzing round, and that Dunning and Kruger were doing excellent business. And yet barely a day went by when Ribbons didn't announce another cut to the farm's budget, blaming it on more of 'Buttercup's debts' being called in. The daily visitor limit was raised from two hundred to three hundred, and premium tickets were introduced for wealthy patrons, allowing them to indulge in behaviour which, only a few short months earlier, would have been inconceivable on Manor Farm. Adults, regardless of their weight, were permitted to ride Cassie bareback, and children were allowed to fondle the geckos, no matter how young and clumsy they were. Costumes were also introduced again. The alpacas were made to wear tiny sombreros and the rabbits had pink bows tied around their necks. When some vicious little boys attached firecrackers to Rocky's tail, sending the ginger tom spinning across the farmyard in terror, all it took was a few banknotes handed to Curly by the parents for the boys to be set loose on the farm again.

It was also at this time that the sheep's food was replaced with the same fodder the alpacas had been eating. When the sheep tried to rally the alpacas to protest this development, their advances were met with wry, even bitter, refusal.

Once a month Curly would leave the farm in the morning with an empty truck, and return later the same day laden down with tonnes of the dusty grey bullets, which he'd then pump into the larger of the farm's silos. He often had a rosy snout and was a little unsteady on his feet after these trips, which some of the animals thought meant he had paid a visit to the Red Lion, or one of Wealden's many other public houses, and which others claimed was simple, honest tiredness after a long day of work. It really depended which of the starlings they had listened to.

Meanwhile, the behaviour of the starlings was changing. Their celestial performances became more jerky and chaotic, and their interventions in farmyard life more violent and random. Some put this down to the birds reacting to the new bleak conditions on the farm, while others claimed there had recently been an influx of new starlings, of a more fractious temperament than the original flock. Still other animals suggested this change in behaviour might be in response to Whistler who, ever since the attack on the kennels, had taken an even greater interest in ways that they might be directed from the ground. He spent his days trying to corral the birds with sticks, and flags, and even once a leaf blower, operated by a compliant sheep. Although none of these sallies had met with much success.

Perhaps in response to this treatment, the starlings unveiled a new kind of performance which astonished the farmyard. Instead of just descending from the skies to chirrup their thoughts into the ears of the other animals, the birds had learned to conjure up whole scenes before the other animals' eyes. In a fashion reminiscent of the moving pictures so beloved by humans, dozens of the starlings would fly in concert to spirit forth apparitions of cows, dogs, geese and sheep – pretty much any farm animal, in fact – and set them in action to tell stories whose impact was far more powerful than a few whispered words in a few receptive ears. And even though no animal really doubted that these scenes were mere phantasmagoria, there was something so eerily lifelike about the illusion that it was also hard for them to believe that the stories being portrayed didn't contain at least a grain of truth.

This period also saw the second attempt by the nanny goat from the WUF to be granted an urgent audience with Ribbons. It was now widely believed that this goat had come to request that Manor Farm allow some of the stray animals from the quarry to settle on its estate, as they were obliged to do by the contract they had signed with the other farms in the union. So as to avoid a confrontation with either the WUF or Balmoral, Ribbons once again ignored the petition. After waiting from dawn until dusk, the nanny goat departed.

Amid all the confusion, it was barely noticed that there were several new foxes on Manor Farm. Almost a dozen, in fact. It was as if, once the gate had been opened to George, once he had been taken in by the animals almost as one of their own, word had got out and others of his kind felt emboldened to show their faces too. By the time spring finally arrived, a veritable skulk had taken up residence in the farmyard – male and female, old and young, highlander and lowlander. Some seemed as tame and refined as George. Others had a slightly more wild look about them, and would ogle the rabbits and hens as they passed, making almost no attempt to suck back their slaver. They were also a roisterous species, who seemingly cared little that most of Manor Farm's species were not nocturnal. At first, the animals had thought they were being awoken by some kind of protracted and methodical slaughter. When they discovered that this tortured screeching was just how the foxes enjoyed chatting to each other, and well into the early hours, it nevertheless inspired a feeling of profound unease in certain animals, with the dormice even talking about abandoning their nest in the spinney and moving to another farm altogether.

Most of the animals, however, just reassured themselves that George had not only caused no trouble since his arrival but, with his dry witticisms and wry observations, had actually proved a refreshing change to the rather arid and miserable grind of the farm since the day of the Whopping Commotion. So there was really no reason to imagine that these new arrivals would be any different.

The summer solstice was three months away – and with it the Choozin. It was becoming increasingly important that the Animalists decided who would lead them against Ribbons and the Jonesists. Despite the damage done to Buttercup's reputation in recent months, it was still widely assumed in the drove that Cosmo would be elected to the post. His only opponent was Pearl, and Cosmo could not believe the drove would be unreasonable enough to elect such a fractious leader. Certainly Pearl was very capable of whipping up a small gang of animals in the yard. But he had little hope of reaching across the entire farm to win Choozin-walnuts from the cows as well as the sheep, the geckos as well as the hens.

From his own pear-crate in the farmyard, Cosmo attacked Ribbons: 'You sweat and toil, while he and the dogs get fat off the profits!'; 'This was once a green and pleasant farm...' Whereas Pearl spent most of his time either singing wistful odes to Sugarcandy Mountain, or denigrating Buttercup. He had taken to repeating several outlandish stories that the starlings had recently played out in the sky above the farmyard: Buttercup laughing and backslapping with descendants of Jones, the human who'd run Manor Farm before the Great Rebellion; Buttercup signing documents for the division of Shore Farm's peat between himself and the greyhound foxes; Buttercup tucking into a roast chicken, a huge spotted napkin flapping around his neck... All of which had been conjured forth from nothing but the birds' rapid movements, and all of which Pearl was now reporting as reality.

Cosmo knew that none of these stories were true because he had received a postcard from Buttercup only a few days earlier. He was currently in Sandbanks, Dorset, staying at the beachside house of an old Whymper contact, topping up his tan, and making good money advising animals from outside the WUF on the craft of a well-run farm. He was writing to warn Cosmo that Whymper and other corporations had recognised the influence of the starlings, flocks of which had also appeared on farms across the county and beyond, and were investing a lot of money in developing ways to manipulate their behaviour. Buttercup concluded the letter with the hope that Manor Farm would do everything it could to protect itself from this kind of influence. Cosmo thought of Whistler, and his clumsy, and futile, attempts to herd the birds, and wondered if the new life of sun, sand and cider cocktails hadn't gone to his old boss's head. The postcard left Cosmo with a dilemma. While it could serve to exonerate Buttercup from the flimsy and outlandish charge levelled by Pearl, that the former First Beast was working against the farm – he also feared that, should the animals hear the warning about Whymper and the starlings, they might laugh him out of the farmyard.

Cosmo's speeches – and only Cosmo's speeches – were also regularly interrupted by the foxes. As soon as he took to his pear-crate George would appear with two or three others of his kind and start making wry remarks, loud enough to put the owl off his stride. Remarks like:

'To pay for everything he's promising we'd need two extra windmills and three new Piles! Or just for his pal Buttercup to pay back everything he stole from the farm.'

And: 'We've heard the too-whit-too-whoo. But when will he tell us the too-whit-too-why, the too-whit-too-what, and the too-whit-too-how?'

And: 'If the fluffy wildling really wanted to be useful, of course, he'd put a stick up his bum and we could use him to dust the farmhouse dining room.' All the while George's scruffy cronies cackled and hissed by his side like tiny hyenas.

The one time Cosmo lost his temper, stopped speaking and just glared at George, the svelte fox looked back at him with wide, innocent eyes.

'I'm so, so sorry,' he purred, before turning to his friends and adding '… for thinking he might be able to take a joke?'

Cosmo decided to ignore the foxes as best he could, and to keep Buttercup's postcard to himself. He was reassured by his firm belief that, while times were strange and hard on Manor Farm, most animals could still be counted upon to make the reasonable choice. And the reasonable choice for leader of the Animalists was him.

Pearl won handily. At first Cosmo was shocked, not so much by his defeat at the hands of the deluded old Animalist, the evangelist for Sugarcandy Mountain, as by his own inability to understand the logic behind it. As soon as the result was announced, he turned to Haw-Haw for his analysis:

'When you have nothing,' the gander said, 'why not vote for everything?' This was an argument that Cosmo could accept, if not exactly agree with. 'Besides,' Haw-Haw added darkly, as he waddled off to see the victory celebrations up close. 'Do you really think Manor Farm is ready to have an *owl* as First Beast?'

Cosmo determined to remain dignified in defeat. He sought out and congratulated Pearl, proffering a wing to shake. The new drove leader looked at it as if it were poisoned, before turning on his trotters and leaving the farmhouse to address the supporters that had gathered in front of the porch early that morning, either to celebrate Pearl's victory or protest his defeat. Many of them were carrying shovels, which they waved above their heads as the victorious Pearl emerged.

'Comrades! Rule by swine is coming to an end,' Pearl intoned, seemingly unaware of the fact that he too was a pig. 'Manor Beasts have had enough of Buttercup's world. Enough of Whymper. Enough of windmills. Enough of the gift shop, selling trinkets and doodads we neither want nor need. Enough of cuts and compromises for all of us, while the dogs live in luxury!'

'Enough of the WUF interfering in our farm!' Flaxen the roe deer brayed. Pearl looked surprised by this interjection for a moment, as if the WUF was something to which he had given little prior thought. He nodded at Flaxen and gave her an equivocal half-smile.

'I have listened to you all, I've gathered your thoughts and your feelings, and I can tell you: most Manor Beasts now agree,' he paused triumphantly, 'that Sugarcandy Mountain is buried somewhere on this farm. All we have to do is dig for it!' At this, a flank of the starlings shot into the air above Pearl, where they began an extraordinary, well-ordered performance. The first scene depicted a more noble and vigorous incarnation of Pearl striking the soil with a shovel. It split open releasing an apparently inexhaustible jet of clover, lump sugar and linseed cake. The second scene showed Pearl distributing these goods to a procession of emaciated sheep, hens and pigeons, while the pigs and dogs, and even a few cows, looked on in dismay. The gathered crowd bleated and oinked and clucked its support; those who had the dexterity to do so waved their shovels in the air.

Pearl had finished speaking and was now being carried aloft by the crowd of animals. Dermott had taken to the vacated pearcrate and was leading the gathered animals in song, the words of which ran:

Friend of the fatherless!
Fountain of happiness!
Lord of the swill-bucket! Oh, how my soul is on
Fire when I gaze at thy
Calm and commanding eye,
Like the sun in the sky,
Comrade Pearl!

And although the final line of the song seemed to slump to a halt, as if a few syllables had been lopped off, the animals sang it with such gusto that Cosmo wondered whether it was only to his ear that it sounded in any way wrong.

few days later, just after dawn, Lionel – the young alpaca who had shared the apple-bobbing stage with Jumbo – staggered into the farmyard, his nails skittering as if the ground beneath him was covered with ice. He was walking with determination and yet a complete lack of awareness about where he was. His eyes were bloodshot and thick with rheum, and he was letting out a horrifying gurgled lament, as though he was being set upon by an invisible predator. He was also painfully thin, his ears were leaking a thick mucus and the fur around his rear-end was caked in manure. Lionel stopped in the middle of the farmyard and began compulsively licking his wool, pausing only to launch into frantic bouts of tooth grinding. Word spread quickly about this frightening behaviour, among the land animals who emerged from their beds to watch, and among the starlings, who took to the sky above the farmyard, blotting out much of the sun's light as they convulsed like a shaken blanket.

It took almost an hour for the Council to act and then it was announced that Jumbo would make an address to the farmyard. Ribbons had recently appointed Jumbo to fill Buttercup's vacated Council seat until the Choozin in June, and had promptly given him the thankless job of Sanitary Officer. Similar to Curly's appointment as Quartermaster, this was believed to be a brilliant move on Ribbons's part, intended to neutralise a threat to his authority; to win over the sheep who, ever since the pear-bobbing fiasco, had been vocal fans of Jumbo; and to teach the indolent boar the lesson that running Manor Farm was actually much harder than it looked.

Jumbo walked out onto the porch. His appearance was met with a collective gasp. Gone was the flushed and greasy look of a pig forever battling a hangover. The black hairpiece that until today had resembled an abandoned bird's nest was now styled into an impressive, angular quiff, and he had a pearl necklace around his neck that bounced up and down as he walked. That quiff and necklace meant only one thing to the animals: Traviata, the old Jonesist sow, who was as loved by half the animals on the farm as she was despised by the other half. Jumbo's pearls, unlike Traviata's, were clearly a plastic toy, dropped most likely by a child visitor to the farm, yet the effect was striking all the same.

'I'm going to be honest with you,' he said. 'I believe that this poor creature has been infected with a Lyssavirus, and is now suffering from something like rabies.' His audience gasped again. Rabies had been eliminated form Manor Farm generations earlier, but was still tenaciously present on some of England's other estates.

'How did it get here?' Balmoral asked above the hubbub.

'That is what we are currently trying to find out,' Jumbo said. Balmoral was heard to mutter something about the quarry. Cassie raised a hoof. Jumbo nodded for her to speak. Perhaps her memory was deceiving her, she said, but Lionel's symptoms did not seem to be those most associated with the feared disease, such as paralysis and a terrible fear of water. In fact she'd recently read…

'Am I, the Sanitary Officer, supposed to take scientific advice from an ass now?' Jumbo interrupted, shaking his head. A few of the sheep in the crowd turned to Cassie and bleated at her in annoyance. 'If you'd have let me finish you'd know that I actually have some rather good news to deliver.'

All indications were, Jumbo said, that this particular strain of the disease almost certainly only affected the alpacas, most likely owing to some genetic deficiency the animals possessed. There was simply no reason to think that hardy Manor Beasts shouldn't go about their lives as normal. He certainly would for, after all, was that not the spirit Traviata had taught them?

'I have full confidence,' Jumbo snorted, his voice suddenly a half-octave lower. 'That if each of us does our duty, if nothing is neglected, and if the best arrangements are made, as they are being made, we shall prove ourselves able to defend our farm, to ride out this storm of disease, if necessary for years, if necessary alone. For while times may be dark right now, the fact remains that I would always – *always!* – prefer to be a freeborn Manor Beast, than a Pinchfield pigeon or a Foxwood fowl.' Clive the Bullock had been nodding his head so manically that the tendons in his neck strained. He now bellowed with prideful delight, frighting the dozen starlings from his shoulders into the air. Jumbo went on: 'For as the fifth verse of "Beasts of England" promises…' He stopped speaking, coughed twice, and sang:

> '*Bright will shine our fields and pastures,*
> *Purer shall our waters be*
> *Traviata will inspire us,*
> *Heal the Manor, set us free!*'

The sheep and hens and cows and ducks, seemed not only reassured by these words, but moved. The alpacas, on the other hand, found no comfort in them whatsoever, and one of them asked Jumbo what he was going to do to stop more of their kind falling sick.

The question annoyed Jumbo. Perhaps he had hoped that an inspiring rendition of "Beasts of England" would be enough to stifle any further discussion. He sighed deeply and muttered that whatever was wrong with Lionel, and regardless of the behaviour that made him fall sick, he would receive the very best care

Manor Farm had to offer and be nursed back to health in no time. And with that, Jumbo turned on his trotters and lumbered back towards the farmhouse.

The animals were so bewildered that they paid no attention to the door as it opened for Jumbo. Had they done, they would have seen that there was a light on in the hallway, and that once Jumbo was inside, his chubby shadow was approached by two others – one of them feathered, the other somewhat woolly – closing around him like a crab's claw. No sooner had the door shut, and barely had Jumbo's words about the care Lionel would receive been digested by the gathering, than the alpaca's four limbs shot out from beneath him, like the legs of a collapsing table, and he gasped his last.

A few hours later a fence was erected around the body of the dead alpaca. Martha watched from the roof of the Big Barn as one of the pigs, unrecognisable in his hazmat suit, shaved the body of its lustrous and valuable fleece. Not long after, a red truck with the words *Simmonds & Son* painted on one side rolled slowly up the loke.

APRIL

I

A week after Lionel the alpaca's death, Manor Farm awoke to another horrific scene. Six of the hens had been slaughtered. They had been yanked from the coop in the night, their necks snapped, their breasts rent apart, their entrails dragged out of them and strewn across the farmyard. The dozen-or-so surviving hens were found huddling in the eaves of their coop, quaking with fear and in too much shock to say what had happened. Few of the animals dared approach the bodies. Even most of the starlings kept their distance, with just a couple of the more expeditionary birds performing rapid flyovers so they could share the gorier of the details with any animal that showed an interest. Most of the animals tried to piece together the tragedy based upon what they could see from afar, meaning that soon dozens of different theories were circulating around the farmyard.

Haw-Haw was quick to declare the 'blindingly obvious': that the slaughter was the work of several newly crazed alpacas.

'A further justification, were one needed,' he honked 'for imposing the harshest quarantine upon them!'

Balmoral was heard insisting that 'outside elements' had to be involved, and that the WUF must take a large part of the blame for not allowing Manor Farm to dig the moat he had long argued for. Marguerite the Holstein declared that the encampment of animals on the quarry should be raided and dismantled at once. Where better for the culprit of such an appalling act to hide? As for Pearl, he was heard to claim both that the bloodthirsty and vengeful Buttercup – his former Animalist colleague – had snuck back onto the farm to butcher the hens, and that it was likely not a murder scene at all, but some kind of act of 'revolutionary suicide' carried out by the noble hens to hurry along the time ground would finally be broken in the quest to unearth Sugarcandy Mountain. In short, there was an explanation to just about every animal's taste. Most of them bought into one or the other, while a few of the sheep appeared to believe in all of them at once.

Martha was unconvinced by any of the theories. Steeling herself for what she would find, she approached the coop to investigate. The hens had always been a tight-knit group, who much preferred to gossip and chatter among themselves than spend much time with the other animals. But the moment she saw the tooth wounds in the birds' necks, as well as thickly clawed paw prints around the pools of blood, every feather, every bone, of her being shuddered with an understanding of the fear they must have felt in the seconds before their lives had ended. She forced herself to continue inspecting the scene. The paw prints looked too big for a cat and too small for most dogs. She also spotted a small tuft of rust-coloured fur snagged on the door-frame. How could she not believe that one or more of the foxes was responsible for the slaughter?

When she returned to let the others know what she had found, she was surprised to see Curly standing in their midst, holding forth about the fate of the hens.

'Perhaps,' he was saying, 'it was not an act of slaughter by a fellow animal at all, but something the hens had done to themselves. Have you not heard of the ancient sport of cock fighting? They may not have been raptors for many generations, but the mindless and monstrous violence these birds were capable of committing against their *own* kind was shocking,' he pressed his front trotters to his breast. '*Shocking* to behold. Surely you have witnessed their frequent scuffles? Is it so impossible to imagine that this was one such scuffle that just got terribly out of hand?'

A ripple of acceptance passed through the crowd. This explanation might be untrue for any animal with eyes to see it, but it was, nevertheless, the most reassuring of explanations offered so far, which apparently increased the willingness of many of the animals to believe it.

Just as Curly finished speaking, Martha noticed his gaze flicker towards the back of the crowd, as if seeking approval. George the fox was standing there, licking what looked like congealed blood from his muzzle. He caught Martha's frightened gaze. At that moment, Martha knew. And George knew that she knew. But instead of exhibiting any fear that he might be exposed, he simply licked his muzzle, extravagantly, one more time just for her.

Martha had to see Duke. He had known about the foxes, and had warned her, but she hadn't listened. Not really. Not enough to do anything about them. Now things had gone too far, and she had no idea what to do. If there was anyone who could help her, she thought, it was Duke. She reached the pool, passed her nest, then stopped dead. Five black tail feathers were sticking up from the bundle of twigs, each of them leaning at a wildly different angle. There had never been more than one feather before. The sight of five hardened the ball of dread that had been churning in Martha's gizzard since she'd locked eyes with George. There was no time to waddle around the shore. She dipped her head, ran, beat her wings and flew across the pool, towards Duke's nest.

She saw him before she landed. He was lying on the shore, his heels in the water, webbed toes fanning the sky. His beak was skewed open and a patty of damp leaves was pressed down over his eyes.

'Duke!' she said. 'Can you hear me?' The old gander emitted a long, tortured groan, and retched, but nothing came out. Then he sat up, shaking the leaves from his eyes.

'It's worse, much worse than we thought,' he drawled, his words more slurred than usual.

'I know,' Martha said. 'The foxes. You were right.'

'Oh, if it were only the foxes!'

'What do you mean?' Martha asked, the ball of dread bouncing hard against her insides.

'My compass has been hurting for weeks,' he said, touching his head with his wingtip. Like all geese, Martha often felt the pull of her own compass, but she had never imagined it could hurt. 'Like it's being torn apart.' Duke went on. 'From the inside.'

'I don't understand,' Martha said. She took a step back, and looked at Duke. His wings were ragged and oily, his eyes were crusty with rheum, and his mating feathers were thick with congealed droppings.

'Nobody does,' Duke said. 'That's what they rely on. That's how they get away with it.'

'That's how *who* get away with *what*?' Martha was almost pleading now. Now that she was looking at him properly, it looked like Duke was about to pass out. His neck dipped and his head described a full circle before snapping upright again. He glared at her with a look that was at once terror-filled and terrifying. But he didn't reply. Instead he pointed at something in the mud along the shoreline.

Martha's own compass shuddered now. Although she wasn't sure why. She had no idea why Duke was drawing these lines in the mud, or what he thought they meant. She was close to despair. Duke retched again, and this time brought up a patty of toxic green vomit. Her despair turned to irritation.

'Duke, have you been drinking from the pool?' she said.

'You are… what you… eat,' he forced out.

'You told me yourself it was poisonous,' Martha said.

'I needed to understand what was behind it!' he said, and groaned again.

'And I needed you to stop being weird for once!' Martha honked back at him. Duke turned over onto his side. Martha shook her head, turned and waddled off along the shore.

'Pry! On!' Duke shouted after her. Martha flicked her left wing, as if batting those words of encouragement away and into the depths of pool. Where, she thought, they belonged.

Ever since Lionel's death, many of the other animals had looked at the alpacas with a mix of suspicion and disgust. No species reacted with more revulsion than the sheep who, until this year's-apple-and pear (that's to say pear-and-apple) harvest, had lived quite peaceably alongside the farm's other woolly ruminants for several generations. Now, more of the alpacas were falling sick. Those that were still well did their best to hide the extent of the outbreak from the other animals, afraid that their standing on Manor Farm would only decline further. At first, this wasn't too hard. The herd retreated to one corner of the far field, which suited the sheep just fine. And, for a time, none of the sick alpacas had symptoms to rival Lionel's. Most were afflicted with increased forgetfulness and the tendency to drool, both of which could be easily hidden. After a few weeks, however, the forgetfulness lapsed into full mental derangement. Their crazed bleating could be heard from every corner of the farm, while the ceaseless drooling was replaced with unstoppable vomiting, made worse by the beasts' increasingly uncontrollable limbs. From time to time, the most crazed animals would escape from the herd, apparently driven by a primal desire to breathe their last as publicly as possible. Over the space of a single week, seven alpacas died in the farmyard, another three inside the Big Barn itself, and one even made it to the farmhouse porch before exploding in a spastic fit of limbs and bodily secretions.

The Council had been monitoring the situation from afar, but was now forced to act. Jumbo was once again sent from the farmhouse to address the farm's inhabitants. This time Curly was by his side.

'This external disease is killing our dear Andean friends at a disturbing rate,' Jumbo bellowed to the assembled crowd. 'While all indications are that this is a disease that Manor Beasts do not catch, it remains our duty to protect those it does attack. If we don't, who will be next? The geckos? The pelicans? The dormice?'

For this reason, Jumbo announced, he had taken the decision to fence in the alpacas' corner of the far field with barbed wire, and forbid any other animal from coming within ten yards of the enclosure. At least until the illness could be understood. He would also, temporarily, have to halt the right to roam – something that would be much easier, he said, had his dear friend Balmoral been listened to and a moat had been dug around the farm. Regrettably, he added, this new rule would also have to be applied to the sturdy nanny goat from the WUF who, this very morning, had reappeared at the farm gate vociferously bleating for entrance. Visiting humans would still be admitted, of course, to avoid pushing the farm even closer to bankruptcy.

The following morning the pelicans painted a few new words onto the Big Barn's east window. In the column headed ᴧᴀᴎOR BᴊᴀᴄTS, the words 'ᴄowS' and 'ShEEPS' now appeared, whereas in the column headed ᴎOT ᴧᴀᴎOR BᴊᴀᴄTS the word 'ᴀLPᴀᴄᴀS' had been painted and, just below it, 'wᴜP goᴀt'.

Clive the Bullock had not been seen about the farm for some time. When he reappeared, a few weeks after the slaughter at the chicken coop, it became clear why. Clive had changed so much that some of the animals in the Big Barn struggled to recognise him. Whereas before his shoulders had been narrow and round, now they were wide and boxy. His legs were also more shapely and his flanks more muscular than before. Many of the smaller animals were frightened by the changes, not least because there was no way for a cow to grow in this way, and so quickly, without the use of powerful growth hormones, which had been banned on Manor Farm, and across the WUF, for generations. Clive's eyes were bloodshot and bulging, both known side-effects of these substances. He was also wearing clothes for the first time. The pigs always sported human garments, dressing up being an inescapable part of farm politics. But among the other animals clothes were generally considered either an extravagant affectation or an undignified imposition. And yet Clive was now sporting a top hat, a bow tie, ballooning britches, and a waistcoat cut from the red and gold brocade of an old flea-bitten curtain. He also had a walking cane clamped between his jaws. Most astonishing of all was what was hanging between his hind legs. Before, Clive had always displayed a neat little gelding scar, a reassuring indication to the heifers that they were safe in his company. Now a pink canvas pouch hung there, weighed down by two sizeable pebbles. The pouch was tied around the base of his tail and swung from side to side as he walked. To prevent the pouch from falling off, Clive had to keep his tail elevated at all times, and was aided in this by the two dozen starlings who had been his constant companions these past months. Clive shuffled to the middle of the Big Barn, both supremely confident and a little unsteady in his new clobber and the body it showed off. When he was certain he had the attention of all the animals present, he dropped the cane to the ground, scooped it between his front hooves and used it to lift himself up onto his hind legs. Then he cleared his throat and spoke.

'For too long,' he said, in a voice that was newly deep and rough, 'me and my kind have been kept down on Manor Farm. The castration of my brethren at birth was not for our own good, as we have always been told. Or for ensuring relations between bull and heifer remain civil. No! It is, rather, a cruel and calculated practice, inherited when we joined the WUF, and intended to prevent bulls from having our true voices heard on Manor Farm. A farm which, you should remember, was founded by and for ruminants. A farm upon which all other animals are tolerated only by our good grace. This. Changes. Today!' he roared, stamping his right fore-hoof, and startling a passing family of dormice. 'From now on, I will make sure that the lowing of cows is heard above the cacophony of the farmyard. To mark this return to Manor Farm's roots I will be submitting a proposal to the Council of Animals for the reinstitution of the farm's one, true historic flag, which me and my starling friends have discovered.' Of all the peculiar declarations Clive had just made, the mention of an historic flag confused the animals the most. Surely there had only ever been one flag: the Hoof and the Horn on a field of green; created after the Rebellion and embraced by every Council since. Clive was not finished.

'I have also decided,' he bellowed. 'To take a new name. One more suited to the dignity and pedigree of my kind. From now on, I demand to be known not as Clive the Bullock, but as John-Bully-Beef.' And with this, he turned and marched from the Big

Barn back in the direction of the large pasture, launching into a rendition of 'Beasts of England' as he left. Although to some of the animals in attendance there was something strange and unfamiliar about the words:

> *'Soon or late the day is coming*
> *Wealden tyrants o'erthrown*
> *And the fields of Manor Farm*
> *Trod by ruminants alone!'*

The day after John-Bully's début, Cassie and Martha met at the drinking pool. They had long stopped concocting excuses to see each other. Both of them accepted, even if neither of them admitted, that each had become for the other as close to a still point in this manically churning world as they could find. So Cassie would come to see Martha, and would either settle down in the rushes beside her nest, or dip her head to allow the goose to waddle onto her back, after which they would go on a tour around the more isolated stretches of shoreline, often chatting until long after sunset. Cassie depended on Martha's unflinching curiosity, her refusal to accept the stories and theories peddled by the pigs… and some of the other geese. And Martha depended on Cassie's steadfastness in the face of an apparently endless, and certainly thankless, quest.

Both of them had been present in the Big Barn the previous evening. They'd kept their distance from each other, as if to parade their friendship so publicly might be a danger to it, and to them. Now they were together, and Martha was installed at the base of Cassie's neck, one leg hanging down each side, the young goose was less interested to talk about John-Bully himself, than how the other animals had reacted as soon as the monstrous bullock was out of earshot.

She'd seen that the younger bullocks were quite stirred by the performance, copying the twitching of John-Bully's newly muscled shoulders, while seeming almost hypnotised by the swinging canvas pouch between his haunches. She'd also seen the family of dormice leave quickly. They must have been left jittery by John-Bully's ominous mention of the cows'good grace'. After all, their ancestors had been branded vermin and chased from enough places, both farm and common land, to interpret such avowals as a warning. Particularly when coupled with sung lines such as '*And the fields of Manor Farm, Trod by ruminants alone...*' It was likely for similar reasons, Martha decided, that the gecko on the skylight kept her thoughts to herself.

But there had been such a cacophony of other animal voices that even her excellent hearing had been incapable of untangling them. Cassie, on the other hand, was able to move among the other animals in a way that Martha, as a prying goose, could not. And she had done, almost as if she'd known that her friend was relying on her to collect the reactions of the various species.

'Not all of them were as impressed as the bullocks and sheep,' Cassie began, as they set off on this evening's walk. 'The deer were asking if John-Bully had any idea how ridiculous he looked. Nobility, after all, is a quality certain animals are born with, not something a bullock could just *claim*.'

'That sounds about right,' said Martha, flicking her beak disapprovingly. 'What about the sheep?'

'Oh, they were very upset,' Cassie said. 'About how John-Bully had apparently forgotten that all animals were more equal than others. The hens weren't pleased either. They wanted to know what he'd meant by not including *them* in his list of Manor Farm's original inhabitants? Milk, wool and eggs were the three original cornerstones of Manor Farm's success. They were right there on the mural! And the pigeons were just plain angry. They scoffed at the idea that cows were not treated fairly on Manor Farm. Each cow eats several hundred times as much food as each pigeon, after all. And when a cow speaks – or bellows, more like – we all have no choice but to listen.'

'And the pigs? I bet some of those fops were jealous of the hat and britches,' Martha said.

'Probably,' Cassie said, snorting. 'Although they were withering about his idea of reinstating the farm's old flag.'

'That *was* very strange,' Martha said. 'Do you think he meant one designed by... a human?'

Cassie stopped walking.

'Everyone was so busy gossiping that only I stuck my muzzle through the door to see what was happening outside.'

Embarrassment caused Martha's beak to dip. She had been so taken with the kerfuffle inside, that she hadn't thought to follow John-Bully out of the Big Barn either.

'What did you see?' she asked.

'That his speech had set off a bloody battle between the starlings. I've not seen anything like it since they day they arrived. Mobs of them smashing into each other, or chasing down one lone bird, pecking at their eyes, trying to break their wings.'

'That's horrible,' Martha said.

'It was, but that's not all.' Cassie dipped her head. This was an invitation for Martha to climb down, even though they hadn't yet arrived back at her nest. Her compass twitched behind her eyes. Cassie wanted to tell her something, and she wanted to look her in the eye as she did. Martha's legs trembled as she made her way down Cassie's slender neck. She hopped onto the mud, turned round and met the mule's gaze.

'Curly,' she said. 'He was waiting for John-Bully outside.'

Martha didn't understand. What use was this fevered bullock to the farm's Quartermaster?

'And?' was all she could manage.

'He was fiddling with that counter thing he uses,' Cassie said. 'But when he saw that John-Bully was done, the two of them whispered something to each other and walked off towards the pasture together.'

II

The Choozin was a little less than two months away, which meant that it was time for those who wanted to be a candidate for First Beast to declare their intention to stand. Pearl was put forward by the Animalists, and at once announced that instead of wasting his time giving speeches, he would instead devote all of his toiling hours to the much more important task of locating Sugarcandy Mountain and beginning the dig.

'If all goes according to our great plan,' he said. 'The mountain peak will be unearthed before the solstice, transforming our farm, almost instantaneously, into a True Animalist paradise, and the very need for a Choozin will vanish.'

Ribbons had reasonably assumed that the Jonesists would select him as their candidate. He was the current First Beast, after all, and had been devilishly successful in convincing the animals that the only way to deal with 'the mess Buttercup had left' was by the strict imposition of Jonesist restraint. He also knew that, given the choice between him and the fanatical Pearl, many of Buttercup's former supporters would likely Chooz the more moderate pig. Curly was Ribbons's only serious rival, and he would be less of a draw for Buttercup's crowd. And yet, when the drove gathered in the front bedroom of the farmhouse, and the question was asked as to whether any pig or other beast saw fit to challenge Ribbons, it was not Curly, but Jumbo who lumbered forward.

'You can't win Manor Farm with just the support of the dumb sheep and a plastic necklace, you know,' Ribbons scoffed.

'We don't recognise that calculation,' a voiced piped up. It was Curly, who was scrutinising his circular slide-rule as he spoke. A glimmer of doubt passed across Ribbons's face.

'No. You need the cows and the deer, for starters. A few of the magpies. The alpacas too. And none of them can stand you,' Ribbons said.

'*We* don't recognise that calculation,' Curly said again. Then, with an air of menace, he added: 'Besides, you're forgetting the starlings.'

'What have the starlings got to do with anything?' Ribbons said. Curly and Jumbo smiled at each other. Ribbons, a suppressed panic now in his eyes, turned to the rest of the drove.

'Well let's get on with it then,' he said. 'While a few dumb woolybacks may love him, I know that true Jonesists are far too smart to bet the farm's future on a pig in a poke!'

All of the pigs present nodded sternly in response.

The ballot took place at once, in the cupboard under the farmhouse stairs, and was conducted with the utmost secrecy. Which meant nobody knew who chose whom, only that Jumbo triumphed with two thirds of the votes, and so became the Jonesist candidate for First Beast of Manor Farm.

The very next morning, Ribbons had vanished. None of the pigs could recall having seen him after Jumbo's victory was announced, and they might have assumed he had melted into thin air, was it not discovered that his desk and lodgings had been cleared. Then some starlings let it be known that they had seen Ribbons leaving the farm in the early hours. To confirm their story, they performed an aerial recreation of Ribbons walking up the loke, his suitcase swinging in his hand, his chest thrust out and his shoulders thrown back, more relaxed than any of the animals had seen him in months. If this wing-spirited vision was to be believed, he was even humming as he walked.

Buttercup's reputation on the farm had only crystallised, and not to his benefit, since his departure several months earlier. Yet, in the days that followed Ribbons's disappearance, it felt as if the very idea of him, what kind of pig he was and what he had achieved in his tenure as First Beast, was already fading from the farm's collective memory. Even when the starlings began chattering that Ribbons had been spotted on the very same Sandbanks estate as Buttercup, an estate owned by Charles Whymper, the dissolute son of the accountant whose company had caused so much havoc on Manor Farm the previous year, the animals found it difficult to take much of an interest at all.

The Council of Animals was called into session at once, to determine how to deal with Ribbons's departure. With Jumbo filling Buttercup's former seat, but Ribbons having gone, the Jonesists now had ten members, the Animalists had twelve – including Pearl and Dermott, who had not been seen in the dining room for months – and there was Quaver, the one unaffiliated member. As most of the animals on the Council had originally been supporters of Buttercup or Ribbons, Curly tabled the proposition that, with the Choozin only seven weeks away, the Council be dissolved so that the campaign might begin in earnest. The vote was carried almost unanimously.

Moments later, Curly stood again, announcing a point of order. Martha, who was watching through the serving hatch with several of the other geese felt her compass twang as if plucked like a guitar string.

'It is of course highly inappropriate that a farm should be without a First Beast for almost fifty days, until the constitutionally mandated Choozin takes place,' Curly began. 'Since the Council has now been officially dissolved, we find ourselves duty-bound to apply clause nine of article seven of our founding charter which states that, in the absence of a First Beast, and when the Council is no longer sitting, the role of First Beast will be occupied, in a purely caretaking capacity, by the highest ranking member of the former administration still in post. And that animal would be…' He looked down, as if to check his notes, although Martha could see from where she was perched that the page was blank. Curly looked up again, his face twisted into a leathery smile: 'That animal would be… Sanitary Officer Jumbo,' he said.

Martha toppled backwards through the serving hatch, and landed with a crack on the cold tiles of the kitchen floor.

Cosmo expected excitement from the other animals. A Choozin, after all, with its extravagant campaigns, loin-girding speeches and ornate walnut bins, was a celebratory occasion for Manor Farm. But in the conversations he listened to in the farmyard, he found only dismay or boredom.

'Will you be voting?' he heard a lamb ask a young hen.

'Ha! No!' the hen said.

'Why not?' the lamb asked.

'Why bother?' The hen said. 'Whoever you Chooz, you get a pig.'

Something sparked in Cosmo. He rushed to the Big Barn, took hold of a pear crate between his wings and dragged it into the middle of the farmyard. A few passing animals, who had never seen an owl on a pear crate before, stopped to watch.

'I, for one,' he began, 'am not surprised by the candidates of the two old droves. But I am worried. Pearl is a deranged fantasist, Jumbo is a dangerous liar. Neither will bring anything but ruin to Manor Farm. Ever since the starlings arrived, the firm foundation of truthfulness upon which our farm has operated since the Rebellion has been shifting about like sand beneath our feet. Many of the *pigs*,' to his own surprise he found himself spitting the word, 'seem to prefer things this way. It lets them believe what they choose, rather than what is real. But it is also tearing us apart. Just look at the Big Barn,' he said, pointing his wing at the east wall. The small group of animals listening to his speech turned to look. Several more words had recently appeared: 'pelicans' and 'Buttercup' now sat in the NOT MANOR BEASTS list, while the words 'most pigs' had been squeezed in at the very top of the other column. 'I believe,' Cosmo closed his eyes in rapture as he approached the end of his spontaneous speech, 'deep down, that most of you remain reasonable creatures, and that you deserve the chance to select a reasonable First Beast to represent you. I hearby announce that I, Cosmo, your loyal and faithful erstwhile Quartermaster will contest the upcoming Choozin. This time,' he said opening his wings wide, 'and for the very first time… let's not Chooz a pig!'

Cosmo had been so caught up in the excitement of his per-oration that he had not paid any attention to his audience. So he was surprised to see, when he opened his eyes, that only one animal had listened until the end. Cassie was smiling encouraging-ly at him as she munched on a long stalk of hay. Dunning and Kruger were there too. Although they seemed more interested in Cassie's legs than in anything he'd had to say. Indeed, Cosmo noticed they were scrutinising the mule with a curious intensity, whispering to each other and smiling. The rest of his audience, Cosmo realised with dismay, had peeled away during his speech. Most were now watching a mob of starlings spirit forth visions of a few famous WUF politicians in varying states of undress.

MAY

I

A few days after the Council was dissolved, Martha was visited in her nest by Scout the starling. Following the slaughter at the chicken coop, and her fight with Duke, she had decided that she needed more allies. And, deciding to trust the flighty bird, she asked Scout to recruit half a dozen more birds to act as her eyes and ears about the farm, surveilling the yard, the outlying fields and the gate, for any sign of suspicious activity. This morning, Scout had come with two such signs.

The first concerned Whistler the magpie, who had been spotted at the farm gate the morning before, meeting with a human in a wide-brimmed hat and a long brown overcoat. After a brief conversation, Whistler had gestured to a thick stack of banknotes, wrapped tightly in a blue band, hidden behind the gatepost. The human picked them up, and riffled them several times at both ends, nodding slowly. Then he opened his overcoat and several dozen starlings flew out, like a hail of shot in reverse, and quickly joined the sleeping flock in the farmyard. At the sight of this – Scout reported in his jittery staccato – Whistler skipped about with delight.

Then the human had climbed back on his bicycle, and begun riding away from Manor Farm. But when Whistler had hopped back up the loke and disappeared from sight, the human stopped again, turned around and rode back to the gate. This time, no animal came to meet him. Instead, he propped his bicycle on its stand and opened the panniers. Out flew a blizzard of starlings. They first dispersed across the surrounding countryside before each discreetly joining their sleeping cousins.

Martha was struggling to understand what this meant. What was the human up to? Who was he working for? Where had the magpie got so much money? A strange feeling of paralysis came over her. Where should she start? Which thread should she tug at first?

'Is it strange for new starlings to join the flock?' she tried.

'Used to come! Time to time!' Scout said. 'Since Choozin announced! *Hoo!* Hundreds of them! More every day!'

From what Martha could glean from the starling's tickering ejaculations, new birds had surged in from every point of the compass these past weeks, and had been causing havoc among the already fractious flock. She could see it with her own eyes, too, without Scout having to tell her. Perching space in the farmyard, once abundant, was now furiously fought over, while the aerial performances had become heavier and more lurching, and would often wheel out of control, stripping a tree of its leaves or caving in the roof of an outhouse, not by mischievous design, as before, but by clumsy accident.

'So what good are Whistler's new birds, when they'll be mere drops in a turbulent ocean,' Martha said. Scout became particularly excited by this remark.

'If! Actually! Birds!' he said.

'What do you mean?' Martha asked. Scout was so agitated now that he took to the air, flew three circles around Martha's head, then stopped dead in front of her eyes, hovering so close to her for a moment that the tips of their beaks were almost touching.

'At night!' Scout said. 'Their eyes! Flicker!'

Martha needed time to chew over what she had just heard, and so asked Scout about the other strange sighting. Scout told her that several of the starlings had noticed Curly was spending more and more time off the farm, although nobody knew where he was going. He would leave in the morning, and often not come back until after sunset. While there was little particularly remarkable about this information in itself, Martha had been nursing suspicions about Curly ever since the Council meeting when his shenanigans – as she saw them – had led to the installation of Jumbo as First Beast.

'Has he set off this morning yet?' Martha asked.

'Just now!' Scout said.

Martha took to the skies, circling high above the farm. Like all of the estate's geese, she rarely flew more than a few metres at a time – to save her clambering over the dry stack wall of the orchard, or to avoid stepping in one of the cows' gargantuan pats – and the quick change in height left her briefly dizzy. But with a few beats of her powerful wings, she had stabilised herself. With a few more, she had shaken off the initial giddiness. And with a few more again, she was struck by the same thought that always came to her on the scarce occasions she soared hundreds of yards above the land: that she should really do this more often.

She spotted Curly's van quickly, chugging away to the west. She banked, following Curly along the lanes that connected Manor Farm to Pinchfield, Pinchfield to Foxwood, and Foxwood to Willingdon. She was so impressed when she saw the famous Red Lion pub that she almost wheeled off course. She stuck to Curly as the surrounding land turned from well-tended fields into wild moorland. When she had been following him for almost an hour, she noticed that a little way ahead the path disappeared into a thick tract of woodland, in front of which ran a tall fence, topped with barbed wire. There was also a sign, which read: *You are now leaving the WUF...* Curly drove straight through.

Martha's nerve deserted her. She was already further from Manor Farm than she had ever been before. And while she had always believed that one day she would see what England looked like beyond Wealden, today was not that day. She banked east, and flew back to Manor Farm.

Martha waited up late into the night for any sign of Curly. By the time she saw the golden cones of the van's headlights wheel into the loke, even the foxes had shut up for the night. Curly drove the van into the farmyard and pulled up in front of the large silo. He climbed out of the cabin, removed the wooden blocks from his feet (which Martha supposed he used so his stubby porcine legs could reach the pedals), connected the feed pump to the back of the van and discharged several tons of fodder, utterly unconcerned about the awful racket he was making. So Curly had been on the regular fodder run? Martha didn't believe this for a second. The fodder was cover, Martha was certain, for whatever he was really doing. And she was determined now to find out what that was.

Pearl's hunt for Sugarcandy Mountain had finally borne fruit. It hadn't been easy. One group of his supporters had examined dozens of old photographs and were convinced the sacred slopes and plateaus were located somewhere below the southern edge of the ploughland. Another group had found ancient etchings of the mountain in a book and analysed the shadow it cast to determine ('beyond doubt!', they claimed) that the promised peaks lay directly under the small paddock. Yet another group claimed to have received a tip off, although they would not say from whom, that it lay buried deep beneath the hayfield. Each group fought for its own interpretation to be accepted by Pearl and Dermott, accusing the other groups of being 'Buttercup's stooges' or 'secret Jonesists' so as to cast doubt on the legitimacy of their claims.

No agreement had been reached after several days of furious debate. In the spirit of comradely compromise, Pearl proposed that each group was equally right, and that Sugarcandy Mountain must therefore lie equidistant from the three proposed spots. When this was plotted on a copy of the deeds to Manor Farm, it was finally decreed that Sugarcandy Mountain was, beyond doubt, to be found buried under the north-western corner of the spinney. No one was entirely happy with this conclusion, but they were at least reassured that while their proposition had not been followed, neither had the propositions from their treacherous rivals.

And so, one sunny morning in early summer, Flaxen the roe deer, sporting a new silk bandana on her head and elaborate daubs of war-paint on her flanks, formed a digging committee which marched on the spinney with axes and shovels humming 'Comrade Pearl' as they walked. There was a nervousness among some of the committee, although they did their best to conceal it. The spinney was known to be teeming with all manner of dirty grubs and insects, as well as larger animals like the ill-mannered, anarchic squirrels and several untamed species of bird. The kind of beasts that all the Animalists claimed to represent and defend, and yet few had ever really met. Which was why many of Pearl's supporters were relieved to discover that the corner they sought was actually home to one of the spinney's more docile inhabitants, Manor Farm's colony of edible dormice.

Flaxen told the dormice that, in the spirit of comradeship and solidarity, they should vacate their nests at once, so that tree-felling might begin. The dormice refused, to the roe deer's utter bafflement. Did they not believe in fairness and abundance for all, Flaxen asked? Were they not committed to a farm upon which it was Sunday all week long? The dormice replied that yes, they most certainly did and most certainly were, but could not see why all of that wasn't possible without destroying their nests, felling their trees, and digging a pit in the ground.

At this Flaxen ordered the digging committee to advance on the trees with their saws and axes. The terrified dormice clung to their nests for as long as they could, hopeful that Pearl or Dermott would appear and call off their mob. When this didn't happen, and the trees began to teeter, the dormice scattered to the three unfamiliar corners of the spinney. Within a few hours all the trees had been felled, and a delegation was sent to deliver the happy news to the rest of the animals on the farm. It was met with joy from a few, anger from some and confusion from many.

The following morning, when Pearl shuffled into the farmyard, he was surrounded by half a dozen geese:

'How can you justify the destructive actions of your followers?' one of them honked.

'What do you say to those animals who see echoes from Napoleon's time in your treatment of the dormice?' asked another.

At first Pearl looked taken aback by the questions. Then bemused. Then indignant.

'I gave them strict instructions to lay down their saws and shovels!' he said, loosing thick cords of saliva as he spoke. Before adding: 'Or words to that effect.'

When the geese pressed him, Pearl admitted that he couldn't remember precisely what he'd said when word had reached him of the confrontation in the spinney. He was, after all, a pig of a certain age. But as a long-term defender of the rights of *all* oppressed animals, it was simply impossible for him to imagine that he *hadn't* vociferously defended the rights of the dormice to live undisturbed. When asked how he might make it up to the dormice, Pearl smiled and said that the only way to honour their sacrifice would be to continue digging for Sugarcandy Mountain. After all, the dormice would benefit alongside all the other animals when it was unearthed.

'Which is why,' Pearl concluded, misty-eyed suddenly with self-belief. 'This very morning, I am giving the instruction for digging to begin immediately.'

Cosmo's speeches in the Big Barn were sparsely attended, and nobody was cleaning the smeared leavings from his policy broadsides – but the owl himself was increasingly confident. Not only did he have the best slogan ('LET'S NOT CHOOZ A PIG!'), and not only had Pearl decided to spurn the vote in favour of the fanciful quest to discover a mountain under the spinney, but the Jonesists had selected the most openly mendacious pig ever to be farrowed on Manor Farm as their candidate to be First Beast.

Campaigning under the slogan 'BUY A PIG IN A POKE!', Jumbo's pitch was that Manor Beasts had been let down by the more conventional of his kind, and so had little to lose in taking a chance on him. He had promised an extra day of leisure per week to the sheep and told the hens that at least half of their eggs would be allowed to hatch. At the same time he'd assured Dunning and Kruger that they would be free to sell the farm's produce (whether electricity, eggs, wool or milk), to farms within and beyond the WUF, entirely free of restrictions. He'd also committed to adopting John-Bully's manifesto for bovine rights, as well as the historic flag he'd unearthed.

More worryingly, Jumbo had started repeating the old Jonesist line that sheep were best when they were sheep, cows when they were cows, pigs when they were pigs, and so on, while geckos, and alpacas and dormice were best when they were kept as far away from Manor Farm as possible. Those animals in the farmyard Set who thought species had been done away with were not only deluded, Jumbo claimed, but dangerous to the integrity of the farm. Cosmo found these views most astonishing. The reputation Jumbo had forged during his time in Willingdon was not only of a pig who enjoyed consorting with geese, cows, deer and even humans, but one who actively sought them out, and not just for their conversation if the 'do-anything-to-anything' rumour was to be believed.

All of which meant that Cosmo was certain that when the animals heard Jumbo's contradictory views, they would turn against him at once. And when they did, where else could a reasonable animal turn but to Cosmo? And okay – so it was true: no animal had so far publicly declared their support for him. But he was convinced that once that happened, once even one animal broke their silence, the traditional binary of the Animalists and Jonesists would collapse and the support of all right-thinking animals would surge his way like fodder from a punctured silo. The most likely to be convinced were the magpies, the very custodians of reason itself! And it was with this in mind that Cosmo paid a visit to the harness room.

The harness room was occupied by the magpies, who had long provided a rigorous education to Manor Farm's piglets in exchange for an exemption from hard labour. The magpies not only had brains to rival those of the pigs, but their capacity for flight was believed to give them a dimension of thought inaccessible from the ground, making them a valuable source of counsel when a complex decision had to be made. And while they had been responsible for some outlandish ideas in their time, Cosmo still believed that they, like him, valued truth and reason above all else.

The first sign that he might be wrong came when he found the harness room door swinging free of its clasp. He knocked, received no reply, and went in.

Cosmo was stunned by what he saw. Hundreds and hundreds of mirrors dangling from the eaves, scratched and patinated, and covered in a thick layer of dust. The magpies' fetish for mirrors was well known. Whereas the other animals found the visions these metal plates contained either entirely uninteresting or utterly terrifying, the magpies found them fascinating, and were known to seek them out with the same avidness with which the sheep sought out beer. And yet, they had always kept this attraction under control. Or so Cosmo had thought. Now he saw that the harness room was packed with hand mirrors and wall mirrors, angular wing mirrors snapped from cars, and huge oval mirrors lifted from dressing tables, that must have taken several dozen magpies to carry and hang. There were also countless glistening shards, planted in the ceiling like the icicles that formed beneath the farmhouse gutters in winter. The harness room had become a shifting labyrinth of reflective surfaces, a confusing and perilous place, entirely given over to the magpies' addiction.

And yet the magpies themselves were nowhere to be found. Cosmo remembered this place as being alive with learned cawing. Now it was silent. He explored as best he could, trying to wend around the mirrors, calling out to know if any of the birds were there. He was about to give up when he bumped into a looking glass, sending it swinging. Suddenly, with an agitated fluttering and a pained squawk, a solitary magpie stood before him.

It was Roussel. When Cosmo had been a scholar (the first wild animal ever to receive magpie tutelage) Roussel had been a young, plump, cocky bird. But the years had not been kind to him. His plumage had dulled and his eyes were cloudy with cataracts.

'What happened?' Cosmo asked, unsure whether he meant to the harness room, to the other birds, or to Roussel himself. The magpie snickered.

'Gone!' he said.

'All of them?' Cosmo asked.

'All of them.'

'Where?'

'To the dogs, or the pigs. Or like young Whistler, to live decadent lives in the copse.'

'But why?'

'The farm turned away from us,' Roussel said. 'So we turned away from the farm.'

'You stayed,' Cosmo said, and Roussel snickered again.

'These mirrors won't clean themselves. So... if you don't mind?'

This was clearly his cue to leave, but Cosmo didn't move. Instead he told Roussel about his plan to unite the farm around a new drove, and his hope that the magpies would help him do this. The elderly magpie, who had been listening with some impatience, shook his head.

'It is our role to observe and advise, not to choose sides,' he said. 'And anyway, however do you expect to win, when it's so much easier to unite the animals *against* something than *for* it?'

Cosmo told Roussel that he still believed, despite everything, that the majority of animals could still be called upon to be reasonable. Roussel cackled meanly, then said, 'What is reason?'

'The ability to make choices,' Cosmo said, feeling once again like Roussel's student, but confident in his response. 'Logically, based on past experience.'

Roussel nodded vigorously, although less in agreement, and more as if he was satisfied that Cosmo had fallen into his trap.

'In which case,' the old magpie said, 'surely the least reasonable thought of them all is to expect your fellow animals to be reasonable… seeing as that conclusion isn't based on any past experience whatsoever.'

And with that he disappeared into the tinkling forest of reflective glass.

II

It was a Sunday evening in early summer. The ground around the alpaca enclosure had been disinfected, the pelicans had been counted and locked in their cages, the last of the stray animals had been rounded up and returned to the quarry, and the security lights around the windmill, kennels and farmhouse had been turned on. Another long week on Manor Farm was over.

Now there was a fluttering and stirring across the farm as beast and fowl alike began converging on the Big Barn. The room was soon packed. Jumbo was going to speak. As Rocky had not shown his face since the disastrous pear-bobbing session, these pear-crate harangues were the only entertainment on the farm. Even those who claimed not to support Jumbo, who claimed to know that every other word he spoke was a lie, came along for the distraction the pig provided.

The audience tonight was strictly divided by species. Sheep stood with sheep, cows with cows, and hens with hens. It was strange to think that less than a year ago, when Buttercup celebrated his sixth Choozin victory, most of the animals would have found the idea of separate pens for each species quite ridiculous. And yet most of the animals present tonight didn't mind the separation. Although mixing had been encouraged for generations, many of them admitted that they still felt happiest when they stayed with their own kind. The only ones to care were the farmyard Set, for whom mixing was a way of life, but they'd never support Jumbo anyway. The geese were stuck in a pen near the very back of the room. This imposed indignity put many of them off, and indeed Martha was the only one to come to the speech tonight. Except for Haw-Haw. Jumbo allowed him to watch from the gallery. The dogs, Dunning and Kruger, were there too. Also on the gallery, curled up in a pair of matching velour beds. They had a perfect view of the raised platform, although they seemed less interested in what was about to transpire there than on something behind Martha. She turned to see Cassie entering the Big Barn. When they saw Cassie, Dunning and Kruger snarled something to each other, and licked their lips, like a pair of hunting dogs identifying their prey. Curly stood in the shadows at the edge of the raised platform, looking from his circular slide-rule to the crowd and back again, frowning as he performed a succession of fiddly calculations. Meanwhile, the roe deer, who never normally stooped to politics, had been ushered through like important guests, and positioned at the very front of the room, just below the raised platform. There was also a fox enclosure for the very first time. About a dozen of them had arrived early and were already quite drunk. As they waited for Jumbo to arrive they shouted insults at the sheep and snarled lasciviously at the hens – although always with an ironic edge, which meant the butts of their jokes had to laugh along or risk being deemed humourless Animalists. Something else had changed which unsettled Martha almost as much as the presence of the foxes. Since the raised platform backed onto the east window, she was able to read the lists, as the last of the light faded from the sky. A new word had been added in the righthand column. It was not in red like the other words, but in bright Animalist green: DORMICE.

John-Bully was also there, in full costume. He was carrying a flag, strapped to his belly by a leather harness. It depicted the silhouette of a portly human in tails and britches, against a red background decorated with four gold curlicues. For some reason, an unfurled banner behind the silhouette contained the words 'TRADE' to the left and 'MARK' to the right. All of which served very well to distract from the quite zealous glimmer in John-Bully's eyes and the peculiar shoulder twitch the cow had apparently developed.

'I'm sure I've seen that somewhere before,' Cassie piped up beside Martha. Both of them had always instinctively sought to protect their friendship by avoiding being seen together at gatherings in the farmyard or Big Barn. But there Cassie was, standing right beside the goose pen. Had something happened?

'The flag, do you mean?' Martha said, trying not to show her concern. 'I suppose the human must be Farmer Jones.'

'No, I don't think that's right,' Cassie said. 'If only I could remember. I've seen so much at the quarry these past months that it's hard to...' she trailed off.

John-Bully's shoulder twitched again, this time so violently that it shocked his starling companions briefly into the air.

'Any progress out there?' Martha asked, looking up at the mural. Was she imagining, or had it faded a lot this past year? Instead of answering, Cassie's jaw started churning, as if working over the question before she spoke it. After a long pause she said:

'Have *you* ever seen a dead donkey?' Martha could tell that this riddle, whatever it meant, had been troubling the mule for some time.

'A dead what?' Martha said. 'Do you mean *mon*key?' A look of terrible hurt crossed Cassie's face.

'Never mind,' she said.

The lights dimmed and the door at the back of the room clattered open. A flank of starlings swept in, flew down the central aisle and gathered above the raised platform. They began spelling something, letter by letter, in the air. J... U... M... B... O, followed by an exclamation mark for good measure.

Jumbo appeared on the threshold of the Big Barn and the gathered animals erupted in cheers. His hairpiece was coiffed again and the pearls hung around his neck. Except tonight Jumbo wasn't alone. He was accompanied by Balmoral, the patriarch of the roe deer clan. The pig and the stag progressed along the central aisle and climbed onto the raised platform. Jumbo hushed the assembled animals with a swipe of his trotters.

'My fellow beasts,' he said. 'What a beautiful sight you are. A testament to the truth that any harmonious farm is founded on both division and unity. Divided among ourselves: sheep with sheep, pigs with pigs, cows with cows, foxes with foxes. But united against the foes of Manor Farm.' Another cheer from the crowd. Jumbo had been addressing the whole audience, but now he angled his snout downwards so that he was speaking only to the roe deer.

'My friends. We are all aware that Manor Farm faces several grave crises, each of which can be attributed to one unfortunate fact: our membership of the WUF. The terrible disease affecting our guests, the alpacas? We could have kept it out had it not been for the WUF! The algae poisoning our pool? We could have wiped them out with chemicals, but the WUF won't allow us! The miserable animals gathering at the quarry? Trapped there because of the ungenerous policies of the WUF! It's time for the voices of Manor Beasts to be heard at last.' Martha noticed a faint smile creep onto Jumbo's face, as if he was a conjuror about to perform a trick. 'So tell me. Tell *them*. Do we love the WUF or do we hate it?'

The animals' response was clear. Given those two options, and given that they were certain they didn't *love* the WUF, the only possible answer was that they hated it. The Big Barn trembled with the declaration.

Martha didn't quite understand what she was witnessing. Jumbo was unmoored from reality, uttering more lies than he was taking breaths, making claims for which he gave no evidence, because no evidence existed. And yet the animals were swallowing his words like luxury fodder. Did they not realise they were being lied to? Or had they just grown immune to falsehoods and broken promises from the pigs? Since no pig was to be trusted, why shouldn't they at least choose the pig who told them what they wanted to hear... or the one who kept them best entertained?

'But today I'm here to tell you about another scandal,' Jumbo continued. 'After Buttercup ran the electricity market into the ground, he indebted our farm to the WUF as well. Since then, Foxwood and Pinchfield' (shouting and booing from the barn floor), 'hopping mad with jealousy at the natural dynamism and innovation of Manor Farm, have been doing everything in their power to prevent Manor Farm from getting back on its own four feet. You've all seen the new black cables that run from the windmill, I'm sure. Well, what if I was to tell you that they do not serve to increase the electricity we can export but instead channel it directly to the WUF, to service our so-called debts? What if I was to tell you that?'

Was he telling them that? Martha couldn't quite be sure. The other animals didn't share her doubts. They were now busy bellowing and hissing their contempt for the WUF (a contempt they had first articulated only minutes earlier).

'I'm here to tell you: not anymore! Your potential will be held back no longer.' Jumbo had reached his climax. He gripped the pearls around his neck. 'Under my Council, Manor Farm will see a renaissance to match, in scale and ambition, what Traviata did with our windmill precisely twenty-five glorious years after the rebellion.'

Martha felt a movement by her side. She turned to see Cassie staggering backwards, uncertain on her feet.

'Twenty-five glorious years?' the mule was murmuring. It was as if the words had struck her, plum on the nose. Before Martha could ask if she was alright, Cassie turned and galloped from the Big Barn, barging over a crate of fluffy gift-shop toys in her haste. Either Jumbo didn't see the commotion, or just didn't care. Either way, he would not let it interrupt his climax.

'As my dear friend Balmoral has been urging for years,' he said, scything the air with his trotter. 'The time has come to take our power back! To leave the WUF! To dig the moat! And to heal the Manor!'

The roe deer at the front of the crowd were in raptures, churning their forelegs in the air and whickering their support. From the shadows at the edge of the raised platform Curly executed yet another calculation on his circular slide rule. This time he smiled.

Chants of 'Heal the Manor!' and 'Dig the Moat!' erupted from the crowd as Jumbo climbed down from the raised platform. Seconds later, the melody for 'Beasts of England' sounded from the old gramophone, and the gathering of animals began singing at the tops of their voices. Although, unlike before, when they would make an effort to remember at least a few of the words, they now gave themselves over to the moment, and instead of a song, the hymn became little more than an incantation:

Jumbo, Jumbo, Jumbo, Jumbo,
Jumbo, Jumbo, Juh-um-bo!
Jumbo, Jumbo, Jumbo, Jumbo,
Jumbo, Jumbo, Juh-um-bo!'

With this song ringing in his ears, and a satisfied sneer on his lips, Jumbo left the Big Barn.

Martha felt the animals in no mood to disperse. There was a charge that had to be channelled. The starlings formed a fat disc in the sky outside, that shuddered and convulsed like a coin spinning its last. The cows and sheep were pacing back and forth, jostling each other, spitting curses against Buttercup and the WUF. The foxes, spoiling for a fight, tipped over the souvenir carts and fridges of fizzy pop.

Martha didn't know whose idea it was. Perhaps it came from John-Bully, who bellowed something about 'taking the power back this very night!' before leading the procession out of the Big Barn and across the farmyard. Or perhaps it came from the starlings, who commingled into a large hovering arrow against the deep blue sky. Or perhaps there was no instigator at all. Perhaps, stoked to righteous fury by Jumbo's words, the Manor Beasts understood as one exactly what they had to do. And perhaps it didn't matter. Perhaps all that mattered was that, barely minutes after Jumbo had left, the crowd of animals had regrouped at the top of the grassy knoll, behind the dynamo room where a dozen or so of the younger sheep, cows and deer were gnawing furiously through the thick black cables. Martha had followed the mob and was watching with a mounting sense of dread.

'Stop!' she wanted to shout, but the word stuck in her throat, like a bullet of undigested meal.

There was a flash and a sizzle as tooth pierced rubber and came into contact with copper wire. Seconds later, three sheep, one lamb, two adolescent stags, and a bullock lay dead on the ground. Their bodies were blackened to a crisp by the electricity that had been discharged from the wires into their flesh, and the air from the far field to the orchard was filled with the grim stench of barbecue.

For a moment Martha thought, hoped, that this would be the end of it, at least. These animals' blood was on Jumbo's trotters. Surely they would all see that animals had died as a direct result of his goading.

But then some of the starlings – whose eyes, if Martha wasn't mistaken, seemed to be glowing a little – descended from the sky. They made their way through the huddle of animals with perfect ease and familiarity, landing on shoulders, whispering into ears. A particularly furious-looking hen, standing near the back of the crowd, muttered something about the dead animals being martyrs. A sheep piped up:

'This is the WUF's fault!'

'Just more evidence,' one of the roe deer joined in 'that it must be destroyed!'

Nearby animals started relaying these opinions, and soon they had rippled through the gathering from one beast to the next, until Martha could hear the word 'martyr' being whispered all around her. As for the starlings, they had alighted their animal perches and dispersed. Almost as if, Martha thought, they had never been there at all.

The chanting began again. Now the phrase 'Dig the Moat!' was not followed by 'Heal the Manor', but instead by 'Kill the WUF!' Other animals launched into the version of 'Beasts of England' made up entirely of Jumbo's name. As the gathering turned away from the charred corpses and towards the farmyard, Martha looked on in horror. If Jumbo could drive the animals to mindless self-destruction and still somehow come out of it as popular as before, how could he ever be stopped?

*C*assie had left at a gallop, but when she passed from the stuffiness of the Big Barn to the farmyard, the cool air of the summer's evening struck her between the eyes like a hammer. She skidded to a halt on the gravel then kicked at the sky several times with her hind legs, as if fighting off an invisible aggressor. A thought was turning and reforming in her mind. It reminded her of the time she'd wandered into the visitor bathrooms, and saw herself reflected to infinity in the mirrors on opposite walls, her image never quite resolving, never quite revealing itself. All she knew for certain was that she had to speak to the dogs. That they somehow held the key to the puzzle that had been troubling her since the mural was unveiled, the puzzle that had sent her foraging about the quarry for all those months. But what could they possibly know?

Dunning and Kruger had left the Big Barn shortly before Cassie, and she saw that the lights had now been turned on in the kennels. When she arrived, Cassie did her best to stay calm, but she couldn't stop her great belly and flanks heaving as she butted the door with her flat forehead It took a long time for the door to ease open and, as it did, Cassie tried to think of the question she might ask them if they let her. But her thoughts were waltzing too quickly for any one to settle for long…

'What happened in the twenty-fifth glorious year?'

'How do a windmill's sails turn when there isn't any breeze?'

'Have *you* ever seen a dead donkey?'

In the end, she didn't get the chance to say anything. When the door was fully open Cassie was confronted by the frowning, chevron faces of Dunning and Kruger, their black monocle-patches and equally black noses glistening on their white fur like lumps of coal in a snowdrift. The dogs looked briefly surprised to see Cassie, then amused. Then they silently consulted each other, before coming to some agreement with a few simple twitches of their whiskers.

Kruger (or was it Dunning?) picked up something from beside the door. He clasped it in his mouth like a stick. Except it wasn't made of wood, but glass, and had a thin tine of metal poking out of one end.

'Well that saved us a job,' Dunning (or was it Kruger?) said, as the other one reached forward and jabbed the syringe into Cassie's neck.

Seconds later, Cassie lay unconscious on the ground.

JUNE

I

Aweek before the Choozin, Martha was woken by Scout the white-feathered starling tugging at her wing. Curly was on the move again, he told her.

Just as before, Martha took to the sky in pursuit. And just as before, she spotted Curly's van speeding away from Manor Farm as fast its old engine could chug. Past Pinchfield, past Foxwood, past Willingdon and the Red Lion. Curly was heading towards the woodland again, and the fence that separated the WUF from the wilds of England beyond. Although now, unlike before, Martha followed him.

Being outside the boundaries of the WUF felt both enormously significant and something of an anti-climax for Martha, at least from the sky. The crops in the fields were perhaps less abundant, and the roads less well-kept, but what she saw was still recognisably England – green and pleasant enough – and Martha relaxed into the regular beating of her wings.

As she flew, she kept one eye on Curly, and one on the landscape below. They passed signs for counties and towns that before had only existed for her on maps and the pages of books: Hampshire, Berkshire, Wiltshire, Dorset, Farnham, Romsey, Middle Wallop, Sixpenny Handley, Meanwell, Bournemouth, Mockbeggar, Dewlish, Piddletrenthide, and Nether Cerne. Some time later she spotted a sign for Somerset, and the village of Mudford Sock, and in her mind she heard these names spoken in Cassie's resonant drawl. Although so much had happened since that conversation that she could no longer remember why that mule been had so interested in this village.

Martha's thoughts stayed with Cassie for a while. She hadn't seen her friend since that night in the Big Barn, when something Jumbo said had caused her to bolt. Several days had now passed without her paying a visit to the drinking pool, and Martha had decided to go to the quarry to see if she was alright... But then Scout had shown up at her nest, and here she was, scores of miles away from Manor Farm, alone, and still no wiser about where her friend was.

Curly must have seen the sign for Mudford Sock too, because he suddenly braked and turned right, leaving the crumbling tarmacadam of the country road for an even bumpier gravel track. Martha banked right too. They weren't just passing by Mudford Sock, then. Mudford Sock was their destination.

A little way along the track stood a small tavern, black smoke curling from its chimney in dense arabesques. Beyond that was the village itself, and beyond the village was a vast factory of some kind, its own pair of tall chimneys releasing thick canopies of jaundiced fumes into the air. Martha was still some way from the plumes themselves, but their acrid particles reached her nostrils and almost sent her reeling. What were they doing there to produce such a vile, death-ridden stench? Next to the chimneys were several large vats, each of which was fed through the mouth at the top by a huge conveyor belt, a monstrous mechanical tongue, none of which were currently running.

Curly stopped the engine, clambered down from the cabin, kicked off the wooden blocks from his trotters, and went into the tavern. Martha landed in a nearby field and, after catching her breath, discreetly followed the pig inside.

T he tavern was a stuffy, smoky den, in which the patrons formed secretive huddles in cramped snugs, calling out their drinks orders to the thickset badger who was tending the bar. The badger's face was heavily scarred, although his eyes didn't strike Martha as unkind. Martha waited for Curly to take his seat in the corner snug – already occupied by a ruddy-faced human man in a waxed jacket and black wellington boots – before hopping into the booth just behind.

'Took your time,' said the man. 'I wasn't sure you'd come.'

'I'd have been here earlier,' Curly said. 'If you kept the roads around here in better nick.'

'Ah, why bother?' the man said. 'If your lorries ain't big enough so the state of the roads don't matter to you, then you ain't big enough to matter to me.' Curly snorted with mirth at this, although to Martha it sounded forced, as if the pig was set on ingratiating himself. The badger came over with two tankards of ale, and clunked them down on the gnarled wooden tabletop. Curly and the man clanked tankards, sipped at their beer, and exhaled satisfied sighs in unison.

'And what can I get you, young goose?' the badger said, turning to Martha. She froze. How could she have been so stupid? To think she could just sit there unseen. She heard Curly shift in the seat just behind her.

'Um, water. Please.' Martha said. Several of the patrons in other snugs laughed.

'What *ale* can I get you?' the badger said. Curly shifted again. Was he turning round? She tilted her head towards the wall, in the vain hope she might avoid being seen, and mumbled:

'The one that's closest to water, then.' The badger shook his head.

'Thought I'd heard everything,' he grumbled, shuffling off. 'I really did.'

'Same amount as usual?' Curly's companion said.

'Didn't you get my letter?' Curly asked.

'I did not,' the man bristled. 'You better not be wasting my time today.'

'Quite the opposite,' Curly said. 'I'm moving the cows onto your stuff too. Which means doubling Manor Farm's order.'

'Well, blow me,' the man said. 'You really are sure of yourself. A lot of my customers are losing their nerve, what with… well, everything.'

'Don't worry about Manor Farm,' Curly said. 'The new First Beast is clay between my trotters.'

'What about your geese?' the man said. 'They've been causing us some trouble on other farms, sticking their beaks in where they're not welcome, honking about my private business to all and sundry.'

'Our geese?' Curly said leaning back in his seat so that the crown of his head was almost touching Martha's. When he spoke again, she almost felt as if he was speaking directly to her. 'Our geese know which side their bread is buttered.'

Had Curly seen Martha? And if so had he recognised her? It didn't feel possible that he hadn't, and yet he appeared so completely unflapped by her presence.

'Let's get this over with, shall we?' the man said. 'Lunch is almost done at the plant. And those beasts aren't going to render themselves.' They both started rooting around for something. Martha angled her head to see if she could make out their reflections in the tankards hanging above the bar. One particularly large, chrome-plated specimen afforded her a direct, if mottled, view.

'Five thousand Manor Pounds,' Curly said, sliding what looked like a fat envelope across the table.

'And for your personal coffers,' the man said, 'one thousand sterling. Double next time, if your cows take to it.' Martha squinted. The man's money was not in an envelope. Instead it was in a thick bundle held tightly together by a blue band.

'Here's to you, Baston,' the man said.

'And to you, Simmonds,' Curly replied.

And with that, Martha remembered when she had heard of the village of 'Mudford Sock'. And the name 'Simmonds'. It was when Cassie had told her about the poor stray horse who'd settled in the quarry. The one who'd escaped with her life from the meat-and-bone-meal factory.

A distant whistle sounded.

'That's lunch over,' Simmonds said. 'Let's get you filled up.'

'You'll need to empty me out first,' Curly said. Simmonds and the pig stood up and hustled out of the tavern without a backwards glace.

Martha wriggled down from the snug, and her legs almost gave out beneath her. She didn't want to follow them. She didn't want to see. She also knew that she had no choice. She had come too far not to peer down into those vats now. But what horrors, precisely, would she see peering back up at her? She left the tavern by the back door, and sprinted across the neighbouring tract of moorland until she felt the cushion of air beneath her beating wings lift her from the ground.

Circling high over the plant, careful not to fly directly through the acrid plumes, Martha took in everything she could. There was Simmonds, tugging on a succession of heavy levers. And there was Curly, opening the back doors of his van beside one of the enormous vats. And there were the conveyor belts, rolling now, the heavy metal orchestra of their machinery churning out an infernal accompaniment to the scene. And there on the belts themselves, were the shorn and rigid cadavers of seven alpacas – Laurence, Thomas, Iris, Ludwig, Philip, Herman, Miguel and Isabelle, Martha knew them all – being hoisted slowly towards the vats.

Martha wheeled away from the factory and back in the direction of Manor Farm. The horrible, terrifying meaning of what she had just witnessed was starting to become clear. Meat and bone meal. Was that what this was all about? Fodder made from the very same meat and bones that Curly was now unloading from his van, onto the plant's conveyor belts. When the animals of Manor Farm died, their bodies were being ground down and made into meal. And this meal was being fed back to the other animals. Over and over and over again.

But for what? Money? Was it really all that base? And why was the money Simmonds gave Curly wrapped in the same blue band as the wad Scout had seen Whistler hand over to his starling trafficker? There was something else too. One final missing piece. It concerned Simmonds's '… *well, everything*'. Martha felt, feared, that she already understood – and the very idea of it frightened her to her core. But she wouldn't let herself believe it until she knew for sure. Although if she was right… well, the animals of Manor Farm didn't stand a chance.

Martha arrived back at the farm determined to tell the other animals about Curly, and the money, and Simmonds's meat-and-bone-meal plant, and the miserable fate of those poor alpacas. As to what they had actually been eating all these months... Before that, there was something she had to find back at her nest.

Despite being stuffed between a bundle of dry grass and a clod of moss for several months, the edition of the *Uckfield Outlook* that Cassie had given her was still quite readable. It was for the short item about the starlings on other farms that her friend had carried it all the way from the quarry, clasped gently between her huge front incisors, but Martha had found little there of interest. As for the main article about the inexplicable plague taking hold in Dorset, Wiltshire and Somerset, she'd read it, but only diagonally – caught up, as she was, in starlings and skulduggery closer to home. How frivolous those months of work suddenly felt. How wasteful. She returned to the article now, her innards knotted with foreboding.

> *... hundreds of animals... dozens of farms... difficulty walking, weight loss and abnormal behaviour... apparently neurodegenerative... lesions in the brain... massive cell death... scientists baffled... suspected ingestion of infected meat and bone meal ...*

There. There it was. The final piece. There it had been. All this time. And Martha had been sitting on this story like a brooding dame. She forced herself to keep on reading now.

> *consumption of infected fodder... misfolded protein, known as a prion... known as a prion... known as a pri... Known as a...*

'Pry on, you crazy gosling.'

Martha startled. It was as if he had just whispered it in her ear. Duke! 'You are what you eat.' Those had been his parting words to her. He had known. All along. Somehow he had known. She had to see him.

When Martha landed on Duke's isolated shore, she knew at once something was wrong. He wasn't in his nest, and he wasn't sprawled in the muddy shallows. Neither was he on any of his favoured perches, which had become overgrown with foliage as if they hadn't been used for some weeks.

She was about to call out for him when she noticed something in the water, three or four yards from the bank: It was a pair of wrinkled goose feet, branching out of the algae-thick water, grey with death, like two gnarled and rotting trees on a desolated tundra.

Martha went straight from the pool to the farmyard and circled it several times, honking that she had discovered something important that would expose life on Manor Farm as a lie. This, she was sure, was what Duke would have wanted her to do. Don't waste time mourning, but expose the lie, and the liars, tear out the rogues like earthworms from the soil.

The lack of response infuriated her. Apart from one young pig, who startled and scurried off to the farmhouse, most of the other animals responded with a listless shrug, a roll of the eyes, or complete indifference. In the past, any whiff of a scandal would have had them trotting and flying from all corners of Manor Farm to listen. Yet Martha stirred the attention of just ten or so of the farmyard Set, a passing sheep, a few pigeons who'd just happened to be roosting nearby, and only a couple of dozen starlings. And they seemed distracted, submitting to the situation just as a tired old stud horse submits to his hundredth extraction. Even so, she still thought what she had to tell them would jolt them awake.

Martha opened her beak... and nothing came out. She had been so keen to tell her story as quickly as possible that she hadn't given any thought as to *how* she should tell it. Where should she start? With Curly? With Simmonds? With Duke? Should she begin by explaining the lawlessness outside the WUF that allowed monsters like Simmonds to operate? Would they believe her? How could she help anyone understand what a prion was when she didn't even understand it herself? Perhaps she should go back further and start with how, since the starlings' arrival, life on the farm had been fundamentally transformed, so that no animal knew who or what to believe anymore? Or how that was perhaps as much the fault of Buttercup and Ribbons as the starlings, and how their light strokes had tilled the ground for utterly corrupt, entirely dishonest pigs like Curly and Jumbo to take root and rise up? And what about the loose ends? Should she tell them that Whistler appeared to be buying new starlings – robot starlings! – with the same money Curly was bringing back from the WUF, when the theory was based on nothing but a couple of barely glimpsed blue bands and a very vague hunch?

She knew she had to be careful. If her story was too short, she might miss out an important detail. But if it was too long, or too difficult for the animals to understand, how could she expect them to care about it? She closed her beak, took a deep breath, swallowed hard…

Just then, the door to the farmhouse opened. Jumbo emerged onto the porch, carrying a black bin bag over one shoulder. He was joined by Curly, Haw-Haw and – for the first time Martha could remember – Whistler. Jumbo and his companions walked across the farmyard to where Martha was standing. The young pig, the tattle-tail, appeared from somewhere with a pear-crate. He set it down, and Jumbo stepped onto it. It was then that Curly found and held Martha's gaze. She didn't feel challenged or threatened, but instead as if she was about to be taught a significant lesson.

Without a word, Jumbo reached into the bin bag and hooked out the bloody and mutilated body of Rocky the tomcat. He held the carcass aloft for a few seconds and then, with a flicker of a smile, dumped it onto the dusty ground. The animals who had gathered to hear Martha gasped in horror and disbelief, recoiling from the body. Their reaction attracted more animals from the Big Barn, the stables and the chicken coop. However divided the animals of Manor Farm had become, one thing united them: they'd all loved Rocky. And now he was dead. Jumbo cleared his throat and spoke:

'Last night our dear friend Rocky was attacked and murdered as he made his way across the farmyard. While we didn't always see eye to eye, we always respected each other.' All eyes in the crowd were glued on Jumbo, but Martha was looking at the body. Something was wrong. Rocky's fur was glistening with dew and was it… giving off steam? Jumbo had said Rocky died the previous night but, Martha was sure of it, this cadaver had been frozen. But since when? Now that she thought about it, when had she last seen Rocky? Maybe not since the night he'd mocked Jumbo at the pear-bobbing.

She looked around. None of the other animals seemed to notice that something was off. They were too upset by Rocky's fate, and in too much need of reassurance. Jumbo was happy to provide it. He wiped an invisible tear from his eye, pointed at the lifeless feline body with his trotter and bellowed:

'Whichever animal is responsible for this is no Manor Beast, and will be brought to justice.' Without another word, and leaving Rocky there for all to see, Jumbo turned and walked back into the farmhouse.

Later that same day the pelicans added 'rocky' to the list on the left of the east window, and 'rocky's killers' to the list on the right.

A few nights later, Curly visited Martha at her outlying nest. His sudden appearance startled her. No rustling of leaves or squelching of mud announced his arrival. Just one moment he had not been there, the next he was, clutching his circular slide-rule. Instinctively Martha rose onto her feet and beat her wings to fend him off, but the pig only tilted his head and looked at her with bemusement. Then he shrugged, before bowing down and resting his chin on the ground to indicate that he posed no immediate threat. After glancing nervously around to check Curly had come alone Martha asked him what he wanted. Curly replied in a courteous, friendly manner, as if he had recently bested Martha in a game of some kind. A game she hadn't realised she had been playing.

'I'm terribly sorry to come so late,' Curly said. Martha felt that he meant it too. That, despite everything, this pig still placed a certain value on decorum. 'And for startling you. What a charming nest you have here. I see…' He paused for a few seconds as if examining. 'I see it's… the one that's closest to water.' In her head, Martha heard the tavern patrons laughing.

'What do you want?' Martha asked.

'You said you had something to reveal. Before the unfortunate events with poor Rocky somewhat distracted the other animals.' He looked away from Martha for a few seconds, as if examining something on the tip of his snout. 'I'm just curious to know what that *something* is.'

'It's less that I know something,' Martha said. 'As I know… *well, everything*.' Curly smiled at this, almost as if with admiration.

'*Very* impressive,' he said. He didn't look at all perturbed. Martha knew why, because the same thought had occurred to her. These past days, her story had sometimes seemed outlandish even to her, and she could see that it would be difficult for the animals to believe it.

'I have evidence,' she said, at which Curly loosed a bored sigh.

'For every piece of evidence you have, I can produce ten pieces that demonstrate the contrary,' he said. 'And Whistler can get his army of starlings spreading my version before you've even left your nest in the morning. For every so-called truth you tell them, I have a dozen of my own. Less resistant to scrutiny, certainly, but more entertaining and reassuring. Given the choice, and I *would* give them the choice, who do you think the animals would believe?'

Martha was almost too shocked to speak. By Curly's candour. And by how he didn't seem at all afraid that she might expose him.

'So you can see how it would be less exhausting for everyone if you just sat on your little... story.'

'And if I don't?' Martha asked.

'That would be a shame,' Curly said. 'Just as it was a shame that Rocky made fun of Jumbo at the pear-bobbing.' Martha felt sick.

'*Apple*-bobbing,' she said. This fact suddenly seemed important to her, although she wasn't sure why. Curly squinted at her, uncomprehending.

'Oh, who cares?' he said. 'What a waste of such a fine, enquiring mind.'

'I do have one question,' Martha said. Curly stepped backwards, so that he almost faded into the surrounding darkness.

'That's not... how this works,' he said.

'Will you silence me?' Martha honked at his retreating silhouette.

'After everything you've seen, after everything you know, do you really think I'd do anything so... vulgar?' he said. A final step back and he had vanished, so that his whispered parting words emanated from the black that seemed to surge forward and envelope Martha:

'No, no, little gosling. You'll silence yourself.'

II

The week between Rocky's death and the Choozin was one of the strangest the animals of Manor Farm had known. On Monday, Jumbo announced that in order to counter the scurrilous, unfair and untrue stories several of the geese were putting about, it was now necessary to regulate their activities. Of course, Manor Farm was a free estate, and Jumbo would never dream of telling the geese which of them were allowed to honk and chatter and which were not. Still, he did not see why he should actively help those dishonest birds who refused to play fair. Henceforth, he would prioritise certain of the gaggle in his dealings with the geese. For this, Jumbo said – adding 'should I be Choozed' almost as an afterthought – he would create the title of 'Proper Gander', which would afford the bearers unfettered access to the farmhouse and the Council of Animals, as well as a specially refurbished gallery in the Big Barn. The 'Proper Ganders' would also be the only geese now permitted to work in the farmyard, for Jumbo saw no reason why those unworthy of a title awarded for fairness should be allowed to besmirch that most sacred of Manor Farm's spaces. So far, only Haw-Haw had proven himself worthy of the title, Jumbo said. Unlike most of his gaggle, Haw-Haw was a frank talker, a truth-teller, a fair and balanced goose. Jumbo looked forward to the other geese proving themselves similarly worthy.

The other geese were furious. They honked noisily while also plotting what they had to do to convince Jumbo to give them the title. As for the rest of the animals, they barely reacted. In part because this felt like an affair between the pigs and the geese, in part because they had long held their suspicions about the honesty of certain geese anyway, and in part because they'd heard the news in the farmyard from Haw-Haw, and he had given it a rather positive slant.

As well using his role of 'Proper Gander' to regale the animals with stories about their First Beast, caretaker or not ('Jumbo saves a drowning lamb from the sheep dip', 'Jumbo chows down with the cows', 'Jumbo chases the WUF goat from the gates of Manor Farm'), on Tuesday, Haw-Haw also honked delightedly about how the dogs were having so much success with the windmill that a second one would now be built, just behind the farmhouse. Ground would be broken in the coming days.

None of the animals had paid Dunning and Kruger much mind for several months. The outrage stirred by their return to Manor Farm, as well as the discovery that they were living lavish lives of which the others could only dream, had been largely forgotten. The dogs had soon been replaced in the animals' minds by newer, fresher grievances, normally identified by a swooping mob of starlings. And so Dunning and Kruger had gone about their business much as in Buttercup's time, exporting the electricity the windmill produced and selling the electricity they were confident it would produce in the future. Indeed, they were so busy that they hadn't fixed the black cable, which spluttered with furious sparks whenever it rained. Although perhaps that was for the best. Jumbo's supporters had taken to thinking of the sections of stripped cable as a monument to those who had died for their cause, and the dogs did not want to upset the First Beast – caretaker or not – by replacing the cable or taping over the exposed wires.

On Wednesday, word spread that seven of the sheep and two of the cows had fallen ill. The symptoms were very similar to those the alpacas had been experiencing, but since it was known to be impossible for Manor Beasts to catch the Wufflu (as the animals were now calling the mysterious disease) Haw-Haw announced that Jumbo had determined it was a mild outbreak of Foot and Mouth disease and the victims were treated accordingly. When the treatment failed to have an effect, and the symptoms only got worse, Haw-Haw made another announcement:

'It's not that Jumbo was wrong to imagine that Manor Beasts couldn't get the Wufflu,' he said. 'But rather evidence that those sheep and cows now falling victim to the disease were likely never true Manor Beasts at all!'

This confused the sheep and cows whose calves and lambs were now afflicted, especially those who knew that their ancestors had lived on Manor Farm back in Jones's time and beyond. But they decided not to question the analysis in case their own status as Manor Beasts was also called into question.

On Thursday, the two lists on the Big Barn were updated once again. The MANOR BEASTS list now read: PIGS, ~~ANIMALS BORN ON MANOR FARM~~, MOST COWS, MOST SHEEP, MAGPIES, ROCKY, GOOD DOGS, PROPER GANDERS and FOXES. While the NOT MANOR BEASTS list now read: HUMANS, FUGITIVE ANIMALS, JACKALS, GECKOS, WUF GOATS, BUTTERCUP, DORMICE, BAD DOGS, ROCKY'S KILLERS, IMPROPER GEESE, SOME SHEEP, SOME COWS and MULES/DONKEYS. There was still no mention of the pigeons or the rats, although they no longer protested this fact. Best just to keep their heads down and, if they could, to stay off the glass wall. The final addition on the second list also confused many of the animals. What on earth, they asked each other, was a donkey?

By Friday morning, the wall of lists was one of the few still visible in the farmyard. For John-Bully had risen at dawn and, with the steely-eyed fervour of the zealot, had spent the first hours of the day hanging his new (that's to say old) flag from every available gutter, windowsill, drainpipe and fencepost, so that the silhouette of the tubby human peered out from a hundred different places at a hundred different angles. Quite where these flags had come from, and who had paid for them, the animals could not say, but some of the starlings did start spreading word they had tiny labels, with the words MADE IN NORFOLK stitched into their hems. But surely this was impossible. Norfolk had recently fallen to a skulk of Mastiff foxes, who held the other creatures in a state of bondage, forcing them to work long days for little fodder. It was simply not credible that any animal on Manor Farm would commission goods from this regime, and so the starling's claim was dismissed as nonsense. More intriguing was the fact that the face of 'Jones' (as John-Bully referred to the human on the flag) appeared far more stern than many remembered from the earlier version. A severe frown furrowed his brow, and he now carried a walking cane which he wielded like a cosh. Despite this, most animals found the effect of the hundreds of flags strangely pretty, although several of the larger beasts and birds were heard to quietly complain that it made navigation through the farm-yard difficult. One misplaced step and they might commit an accidental desecration.

John-Bully had been able to complete this redecoration of the supposedly neutral space of the farmyard without interference thanks to the complete absence of Pearl's supporters. They had been digging on the patch of land, just beyond the large pasture, that the animals had once called the spinney but which now – given the trees had all been felled – most just called 'the pit'. Work had progressed quickly, with the animals taking shifts from sunrise to sunset. Fuelled by their youthful energy and repeated renditions of 'Comrade Pearl' the diggers were now thirty feet underground, in a hole ten feet wide. Dermott had remained outside the hole and set up a pulley and a rope so that food could be delivered in buckets, which were returned filled with earth. This way, the diggers didn't have to leave the hole to eat, which was fortunate, since the longest ladders on Manor Farm were only fifteen feet long, and most of the animals, apart from a few of the pigs, were unable to use them anyway. The atmosphere down the hole was celebratory. By day the comrades dug while Flaxen, whose hooves were too fragile to dig, did her part singing songs. By night they sat in a circle discussing how much better life would be once Sugarcandy Mountain was unearthed. There was little talk of the impending Choozin. As far as they were concerned it didn't matter. Not when, any day now, a shovel blow would be struck, Sugarcandy Mountain would be revealed, and a new world of abundance and sloth would arrive for the animals of Manor Farm.

Several of the animals had noticed during the previous week that Martha the young Brent goose had been spending a great deal of time in the farmyard and around the Big Barn, despite not yet having received the title of 'Proper Gander'. It was as if she was determined to be seen in public, as if the eyes of the other animals upon her gave her a sense of confidence or safety that she was denied when at the more isolated drinking pool.

'She's gone quite honking mad, poor thing,' Haw-Haw enjoyed telling any animal that would listen. 'She's got it in her tiny brain that Whistler is manipulating the starlings... as if such a thing was possible! And that the starlings, in turn, are manipulating you.' Haw-Haw's audience bridled at this.

Many of the starlings were now also spreading stories about Martha that were much more damning, alighting on shoulders and wings across the farm, and whispering so quickly in ears that often the animals were uncertain whether they had just been gossiped to by a starling or had come up with a thought under their own steam. Martha was taking money from the WUF to undermine Jumbo's campaign, the birds said. She was working with Whymper to steal the blueprints of the windmill. She was even peeing in the alpacas' water trough, and so causing their horrific illness. It was unclear where these tales were coming from, or why a little known and apparently unobtrusive goose was suddenly the centre of everyone's attention. But this did not matter. After a while, the animals stopped laughing at Martha, teasing her when she passed, and instead began shouting insults, calling her a disgrace to her kind and the farm. Some of the foxes spat at her. Some of the sheep turned and farted.

Which was how John-Bully was able to get so close to her before any other animal noticed the crazed look in his eyes and the froth dangling like string from his mouth. After all, his behaviour wasn't too different from those of Martha's other tormentors, his cries of 'Manor Farm for Manor Beasts!' and 'Kill the WUF!' blending, rather harmoniously, with their own. Indeed, the animals that were present when the horrible event occurred would later claim that it was only when John-Bully opened his wide jaws, then snapped them shut upon Martha's thin neck, that the bullock had given any indication whatsoever that he posed a threat. Only when he lifted her from the ground and shook her did they understand that his actions, unlike theirs, were not just a bit of fun. Only when he spat her out like a chunk of half-chewed meal did some of them understood that things had gone too far. Martha had screamed with blind panic when the bullock had lunged, and screamed some more as he had waggled her in the air. But she had stopped screaming by the time she hit the ground.

'Cows before fowls!' John-Bully bellowed, before turning and galloping out of the farmyard and towards the quarry.

When they were sure the danger had passed, some of the animals in the farmyard gathered round Martha's unmoving body to look, and to help if they could. One of the hens prodded her beak into the goose's belly, but she didn't move. A sheep tried to staunch the blood that had been sluicing from her neck, and which had now reduced to a mere trickle, but it was too little, too late. This goose would not honk again. Just as the reality of what had happened began to dawn on the animals a starling with a single white feather landed beside Martha, looked into the black bead of her eye for a few seconds, and then shot up into the sky, higher and higher, shrieking with despair as he went.

Later that day, Jumbo issued a statement, which Curly read from the farmhouse porch. Martha's death was a tragedy. John-Bully, had been captured, restrained and sedated. While Jumbo and Martha had had their disagreements, he respected the sacred work that she'd done and so had decided to award her the title of 'Proper Gander' posthumously, in recognition of her courage and integrity. More than anything, Curly read, Martha was a believer in the farm's democracy and, unlike those Animalists who were now trying to orchestrate a delay to the vote for base tactical reasons, Jumbo and the Jonesists on the Council had made sure that the Choozin should proceed as planned, although now in Martha's honour. Curly finished speaking and handed the speech to Haw-Haw so that he could spread the word. As for his thoughts on the murder, the line was always the same: 'It was a terrible, terrible accident,' he would say. 'If only she hadn't stuck her beak in, she could still be here today.'

On the evening before the Choozin, Cosmo took a stroll around the farmyard, which had been immaculately prepared for the frenzy of the following day. Despite the rancour of the weeks leading up to them, past Choozins had always felt like a festival, a celebration of the fact that, for all the farm's problems, and for all its inhabitants' differences, they still lived on an estate run by and for animals.

Cosmo wondered if this year's Choozin would follow suit or whether the pomp and protocol – such as the announcements on the hour, every hour reminding the animals to exercise their hard-won freedom to Chooz – might feel unseemly, given that the farmyard had only recently borne witness to a gruesome murder. While Cosmo understood and agreed, in theory, that the Choozin should go ahead as planned, it also seemed strange to him how quickly the animals' attention seemed to be diverted from the killing, and how few of them seemed to be mourning the poor goose's death.

And yet, despite all this, and even though so much had changed on Manor Farm since the previous Choozin, it still lifted Cosmo's spirits a little to see the barrels at the foot of the Big Barn's east wall. Earlier that day, he had watched a dozen foxes wrestle them out of the farmhouse cellar and roll them into place. That task normally fell to Cassie. Where was Cassie, come to think of it? He hadn't seen the soft-natured mule for some weeks. He remembered how before Cassie it had been her mother Gypsy… and before that? Some other beast of burden, of whom Cosmo had only a vague recollection.

The foxes hadn't done a bad job, though. The barrels stood upright, the new pots of branding ink sat unopened on the desk, the small stage was set for the various animal choruses that would entertain the line throughout the day, and the yards and yards of bunting fluttered in the evening breeze. This year, the bunting was somewhat outshone by the flags John-Bully had hung a few weeks earlier, and which had been left flying despite his murderous actions.

And there was the large wooden board that announced the rules for the Choozin, positioned on an easel just behind the barrels. For this Choozin, the rickety old board had been retired and a new one made. In truth, Cosmo preferred the old board. He felt that its warped and beaten aspect acted as an ineffable but very present link to former First Beasts and Choozins past. But he also knew that nostalgia and sentimentality were some of the least logical emotions, despite their force, and understood the reasonable advantages of a clear and pristine board. He read it silently to himself, his beak tickering over the words.

ROOLS FOR thE ChooziN

1 bEaSt. 1 waLLNut.

AFtER coLLEctiN thEiR waLLNut aLL bEaStS muSt gEt a tEmpRy bRaNd.

waLLNutS muSt bE dRoppt iNto thE baRREL oF thE choozEd bEaSt.

ALL bEaStS muSt bE FREE to chooz without REStRaiNt.

IF thERE iS No oNE thEy wiSh to chooz. bEaStS may Eat thEiR waLLNutS.

BEaStS who caNt REEd caN aSK FoR hELP FRom a chooziN agENt to FiNd thE RitE baRREL.

No bEaSt ShaLL havE axESS to. oR SitE oF thE baRRELS whiLE thE chooziN iS happENiN.

chooziN bEgiNS at SuNRISE.
chooziN ENdS at SuNSEt.
TaLLyiN of thE waLNNutS iS duN iN thE faRmyaRd foR
   aLL bEaStS to SEE.

It was only on his second reading that Cosmo realised something
had changed. He was sure that the old board had not used the
word 'beasts' but 'animals', as it sought to echo the moral force of
the farm's famous, if somewhat recently neglected, motto – that
all animals were more equal than others. Still, the word 'beast'
had become much more popular in recent months. And perhaps,
Cosmo thought, it was only reasonable and proper to keep with
the vernacular of the times. Besides, whether it spoke of 'beasts'
or 'animals' there was something reassuring about the fact that no
animal from either side sought to question the deep-rooted rightness
of the rules. Cosmo also didn't remember the rule about eating
walnuts. There used to be a barrel set aside for those animals who
were unimpressed by any of the candidates. Although perhaps it
wasn't such an unwise change, given the recent reductions in fodder.

Even though Cosmo couldn't see any logical way he might
lose, the small changes to the Choozin routine, coupled with the
strange and febrile atmosphere on the farm in the past months,
meant he once again felt compelled to plot his path to victory
in his mind:

Point one: Despite the fervour of the sheep, cows and a few
other supporters, the Jonesists still had more than half the farmyard against them.

Point two: Given this, a victory for Jumbo was surely impossible.

Point three: Furthermore, the instant that poor goose's body
had been cast lifeless to the gravel, surely the chance of Jumbo
snuffling back any support was over.

Point four: Surely even Jumbo's supporters would now step back from the line they had been toying with crossing these past months. The line between reason and unreason, between decency and indecency, between order and chaos.

Points Five to Thirteen, and Conclusion: Surely, given that vile murder, and the return of the dogs, and the spreading of the Wufflu, and the madness with the Manor Beast lists, and Rocky, and the slaughter at the chicken coop, and the chaos the starlings were wreaking, and the destruction of the dormouse nest, and the mad project to unearth Sugarcandy Mountain… And surely, given the fact that Jumbo was a liar and a cheat who stood for everything a First Beast should despise… Surely, given all this, the animals of Manor Farm – who were, despite everything, still surely reasonable creatures – had only one choice in the Choozin tomorrow. And surely that choice was him, Cosmo. Surely, now was his time.

The sun had barely risen before Cosmo understood that while the rules of the Choozin were being followed to the letter, the spirit in which they were being followed was something else entirely.

He had not considered the effect that the recent changes in the yard would have on the flavour of the day. For this was the first Choozin when animals had not lined up to Chooz beneath the reminder that 'ALL ANIMALS ARE MORE EQUAL THAN OTHERS'. Instead they had to cast their walnut under the words 'MANOR FARM FOR MANOR BEASTS' as well as those horrible lists. Cosmo had never much liked the new motto, but this was the first moment that he truly understood it had replaced its timeless and unchanging predecessor, and with something much more rickety.

It also surprised him to see that the Choozin Agents were foxes, rather than the disinterested magpies who traditionally handed out walnuts, issued the brands, and guarded the barrels. Perhaps he was wrong to be surprised. If he had learned one thing from his conversation with Roussel it was that the magpies weren't fit for much these days. And nowhere did the rules state that the Choozin Agents *had* to be magpies. Still, there was something about the way the foxes glared at the queuing animals, beating stripped walnut branches against their rough paws, that left Cosmo very uneasy.

It didn't take him long to realise that most of the animals on the NOT MANOR BEASTS list (the geckos, the dormice, the geese…) weren't turning up to cast their nuts at all, despite being officially encouraged to do so. And those few animals from that list who did try to Chooz were being set upon by an aggressive flank of starlings as soon as they entered the farmyard, the birds encircling them with such sound and fury, beating their wings and chirping shrilly, that only an intrepid trickle made it all the way across the yard. Cosmo pointed this out to one of the foxes who looked from him to the starlings, then sneered:

'I can't see any actual *restraint*, can you?' Cosmo had to concede that he was right.

When any NOT MANOR BEASTS managed to brave the starlings and foxes and actually reach the Choozin desks, Cosmo was astonished to see them scuttle away with their walnut and devour it hungrily in one corner or other of the farmyard. As for those animals that were on neither list (the pigeons, rats, rabbits and hens), they had clearly decided it was best to keep their heads down. Meanwhile, the alpacas, as well as many of the sheep and cows, were either confined to their pens, or too busy caring for their sick to find the time to Chooz.

All of which meant that the line to collect the walnuts was much shorter than Cosmo had ever seen it. While they waited, the animals were regaled from the small stage not, as in the past, with a selection of traditional farm ballads, but with only one song, or rather one tune. *Beasts of England*, hummed by a choir of piglets. Without the hook of the familiar, or rather half-familiar text, even Cosmo found it hard to stop his mind singing the version that had become the hectoring campaign song of his rival:

> *'Jumbo, Jumbo, Jumbo, Jumbo,*
> *Jumbo, Jumbo, Juh-um-bo!*
> *Jumbo, Jumbo, Jumbo, Jumbo,*
> *Jumbo, Jumbo, Juh-um-bo!'*

As the day progressed, an understanding dawned on Cosmo, with the slow yet irrepressible impetus of a full moon rising behind the farmhouse on an autumn night. He may have been right that most of the animals would make the reasonable choice on the day. But he now saw that he had been wrong about what exactly that choice was. The reasonable choice for most of the animals was not to face the intimidation of the foxes, or the frenzy of the starlings. Nor was it to spend hours in line when they could be caring for their kin. Nor was it to throw away a walnut that could stave off hunger for a precious hour or two. No, the reasonable choice was to stay as far away from the Choozin barrels as they could.

Jumbo won the Choozin by a large margin. Pearl came second. Cosmo received just two votes, one of which was his own. He had no idea who his other supporter was.

After the Choozin Chief (another fox) had proclaimed the results, Pearl mounted a pear crate in the farmyard and announced that while he may not have won the Choozin, the fact that Sugarcandy Pit now reached a glorious, history-defying fifty feet underground was a clear sign that he and the Animalists had won the argument.

The following day, the seats on the Council of Animals were divided. The Animalists would be a mere rump of their former size. Cosmo would not be seated at all.

Jumbo's control of Manor Farm was complete.

Cosmo didn't blame the other animals for his loss. He didn't really even blame Jumbo or Pearl, although he did hold them both responsible for the result. The only animal Cosmo blamed as he tottered, dazed, out of the farmyard, was himself. He thought about that evening he and Buttercup had spent in the Big Barn, a few months and a lifetime ago, when it first became clear that the foundations upon which the modern Manor Farm had been built were shifting. That evening it was Cosmo who'd understood. Who'd had to explain to Buttercup that change was coming, and it would not be in his favour. What had happened to him in between times?

As he shrugged his wings from his sides, beat them once and hopped into flight, soaring high up into the air, and then down towards the wild copse a mile or so beyond the bounds of the farm, where he had been born and grown up and where he now intended to spend some time reflecting about what precisely had happened, and deciding what to do next, there was one question that troubled Cosmo more than any other: why it had been so easy for him to see that Buttercup was done for... and yet so difficult to see that he was finished too?

The Big Barn was decked out for the Choozin party. The troughs were filled with beer and streamers were hung. And yet, despite having handed Jumbo a resounding victory, most of the animals seemed in no mood to celebrate. Many of the sheep and cows were too busy caring for those that had been struck down with the Wufflu to attend a party, while the animals who had come to the Big Barn just looked stunned by what Manor Farm, by what *they*, had done. The party was mainly attended by a small but raucous crowd of Jumbo's supporters, who were determined to enjoy themselves despite (or perhaps because of) the despair many of the other animals were feeling.

When Jumbo finally appeared on the raised platform, a collective gasp sharpened the atmosphere in the room. For the First Beast Elect was accompanied not only by Curly, Whistler and Haw-Haw, his constant companions throughout the campaign, but also by George and half a dozen more foxes. In his speeches to the sheep and hens, Jumbo had repeatedly declared himself the heir of Traviata, the defender of the farm from the worst instincts of the foxes. And yet now the foxes were not only standing alongside him, but forming a protective ring, like a phalanx of imperial guards. Jumbo, already quite drunk, staggered to the middle of the platform and grabbed Haw-Haw's loudhailer.

'This is not a Jonesist victory!' he slurred. 'We are not a drove. We are an uprising. Today we have overturned the established order and we have done so without a single drop of Manor Beast blood being shed.' Jumbo's supporters met his words with one of the most bloodthirsty screams ever heard on the farm. Jumbo wasn't finished: 'At dawn tomorrow we will begin work on the glorious moat that will sunder our farm, once and for all, from the corrupting influence of the WUF. And to those fear-mongers who say we need the WUF for our fodder, let me tell you that you are wrong. The Wuf may need us, but we don't need the WUF. We, after all, are not Pinchfield or Foxwood. We are Manor Farm! And not only have we just broken ground on a second windmill, but we have also, just this afternoon, signed an exclusive contract with Simmonds, to supply all of our fodder. Simmonds! The finest supplier of fodder in the whole of England! This would have been impossible if we were still under the thumb of the WUF!' Jumbo lowered the loudhailer and, from a bucket that had been discretely placed beside him, scooped up a handful of the crumbly grey meal. He help it aloft, and opened his mouth ready to guzzle it down. 'Take it from me. Simmonds's fodder is healthier, tastier and...'

'Poisoned!'

It wasn't just the interruption that caught all the animals by surprise, but the strange accent in which it came. Standing on the threshold was the hairy, stocky frame of the creature who had come to be known as the Wufgoat. Jumbo squinted. Then, recognising the nanny goat, he sneered.

'Extraordinary!' he said. 'Even now, they cannot accept our victory.'

His supporters hollered. Three of the foxes left the raised platform and started making their way towards the intruder. She was doughty, however, and now she had made it this far she would not be stopped.

'The WUF has been investigating Simmonds's for months,' she said. 'We believe that something in their fodder is causing the terrible disease affecting Manor Farm. We have already forbidden it from every other farm in the WUF. This is what I have been trying to tell you.'

The sturdy goat held out a piece of paper. All the animals present, from the supporters on the floor, to the pigs on the raised platform squinted to see what she was showing them.

'Our experts…' she began.

'Experts?' spat Curly. He had taken hold of Haw-Haw's loud-hailer now. 'Do you really expect us to believe those meaningless squiggles you're holding up are the work of *experts*?'

A ripple of laughter washed over the gathering. Each of the animals had been squinting at the squiggles on the goat's piece of paper, and each of them had been worried that they alone didn't understand what they represented. What an extraordinary relief it was, then, to hear another animal – and not just any animal but a pig, and not just any pig but Curly, the smartest of *all* the pigs – declare them to be nonsense. And now that they looked again, they could see clearly that he was right! Of course the squiggles were meaningless! At least they were to all the animals on Manor Farm, except for two geese – one Brent, one Greylag, both now dead. The laughter ramped up from chuckles of consolation to something that sounded more like goading.

'They're prions,' the goat tried. 'Misfolded proteins, caused eating the repurposed…'

'You're wrong,' Jumbo grunted. He had taken the loudhailer back. 'Simmonds's comes from Somerset, where we have many more loyal friends than Pinchfield and Foxwood. If the fodder was poisoned don't you think they'd have told us? And besides, the deal is signed.'

The goat nodded.

'If you are so sure Simmonds's fodder is safe,' she said, 'then eat some.'

Jumbo looked at the grey bullets piled up in his trotter. Doubt flared across his face. A muttering rose from the floor of the Big Barn. Doubt, as the new First Beast well knew, was infectious.

'I'll do better,' Jumbo said. He lowered the loudhailer and jabbed a trotter at something behind the raised platform. A few seconds later a piglet was lifted onto stage. 'My daughter,' he said. Curly whispered something in his ear. 'Appolline. The…' Jumbo grimaced, as if at the wasted opportunity for a joke. 'The *pear* of my eye.'

Jumbo was known to have fathered anywhere between five and seven litters of pigs since his return. With a litter producing an average of eight pigs, that meant there were about sixty of Jumbo's offspring growing up on Manor Farm, and this was the first time any of the animals could remember that Jumbo had ever acknowledged their existence.

Little Appolline looked nervously about, dazzled by the light and the crowd amassed before her. Curly gestured to two of the foxes, who pounced on the piglet, pinning her to the boards. The tiny creature squealed with terror as a third fox propped her mouth open with a splint. Jumbo approached, looming over her, the trotter of fodder still held aloft.

'Answer me this,' Jumbo said, puffed up with indignation. 'If I was not entirely, completely, totally, convinced of the safety of Simmonds's fodder, do any of you really think I would do this?'

He stuffed the meal into the writhing piglet's mouth. Jumbo's supporters cheered, as if the definitive blow in the argument had been struck. Even those who were not supporters of the new First Beast had to admit that no normal parent would take such a risk. The piglet, still quaking with terror, was removed from the platform and the pear-bobbing barrel was rolled into place. None of the animals noticed four other foxes surrounding the Wufgoat and leading her roughly from the Big Barn.

Later that same evening a second, private party was thrown in the farmhouse. By nightfall loud laughter and bursts of singing could be heard across the farm. A small gathering of animals decided to creep as quietly as possible into the farmhouse garden so they could take a peek at the festivities. At the gate they paused, half frightened to go on, but Marguerite the aged Holstein led the way in. The animals tiptoed up to the house, and those that were tall enough peered in at the dining-room window. The only light in the room was from the dim embers of a long-neglected fire, so the animals at the window did not want to believe too much in what they thought they saw, in case their eyes were deceiving them. Nevertheless, there, round the long table, they were certain they could make out Dunning and Kruger, Haw-Haw, George the fox and, to their amazement, John-Bully, free of any restraint or sedation. There were also several humans, including one who looked very much like the man from Whymper Associates, whose car the animals had destroyed on the day of the Whopping Commotion. In the middle of the table were piles of banknotes, both Manor Pounds and other unfamiliar currencies, as well as blueprints that appeared to be the design for a dynamo of some kind.

What most surprised the animals, more even than the presence of the goose-murdering bullock, was that it was not Jumbo sitting at the head of the table, but Curly. The new First Beast was nowhere to be seen, and the furry Baston looked very much like he was holding court. It was Curly who was pouring the wine, Curly who was handing out cigars, Curly at whose jokes the guests laughed a little too loud and a little too hard. At one moment, when a hush had fallen on the gathering, Curly raised his glass and spoke.

'To Jumbo,' he said with a sneer. 'The founder of this feast.' The other guests laughed and raised their glasses too.

'How did you manage it?' one of the humans, whose nose was reddened with drink, asked the Quartermaster.

Curly flashed a satisfied smile and took a brown envelope from under the table. From it he removed a dozen photographs which he scattered across the table. The animals at the window could not make out what the photos showed, but the gathering broke out in hoots of laughter.

'So the stories are true!' one of the humans said with a guffaw.

'And now he's in place?' the human from Whymper asked now. 'How will you control him?'

Curly smiled.

Just as the animals at the window thought they had seen everything, but understood nothing, a gust of wind enveloped the farmhouse, barrelled down the chimney and blew across the embers, for a second or two casting a brilliant orange glow over the room. Those animals who happened to be looking in just the right direction at just the right time, saw something in the dark beyond the pantry door that startled them: Jumbo, naked as the day he was farrowed, trying to mount a bored-looking gilt. She was got up in lipstick and a frizzy blonde wig, and had upon her shoulders a huge chocolate cake, in which the new First Beast proceeded to bury his snout.

SOME TIME LATER...

Each day in the dynamo room was more or less the same. The sun would rise, projecting a dim lozenge of light onto the opposite wall, which would then creep downwards, getting brighter and brighter, as it approached the ground, before disappearing entirely some time towards the middle of the morning. Soon after that, an electric bolt would jolt open, and a dog would ease the door ajar, toss in a bale of hay or straw, make some kind of disobliging comment about laziness or manure, then leave.

Benjamin the donkey had long ago lost count of how many days had passed since he'd been coaxed there. Hundreds certainly, thousands more likely. Traviata had persuaded Benjamin that moving him from the stable was not only necessary for the prosperity of the farm, but also for his own health. He would be fed regularly and well, and would be protected from the inclement English weather, which would be harder and harder for his joints to bear as he aged.

'What if I like the inclemency?' Benjamin had countered, but Traviata had appeared not to hear him. What Benjamin had not said was that while the stable might be damp and draughty, it was also home to Gypsy, the most beautiful mare he had ever seen. It was the first time he had ever allowed himself to think there may be a companion for him on Manor Farm. Gypsy nudged up against him when the nights grew cold, and when she nickered she showed off the most extraordinary, toothy smile. It was such a strange match, Gypsy's noble bearing and Benjamin's glum countenance, that some of the other animals joked that, if they ever had a molly together, they should name her Cassandra after the admirable but gloomy, and least-listened to of human goddesses. Gypsy was well into her twenties, so far more aged than most of the other animals. But she was not as old as Benjamin. And it was because of his new desire to stay around for as long as possible, to spend as much time with her as possible, that Benjamin let himself be charmed by Traviata's talk of an easier, gentler existence.

From then on, Traviata had continued, the lucky donkey would have one job; making sure the dynamo kept spinning when the wind dropped. Benjamin had never believed Traviata's more extravagant promises. Donkeys, as he'd liked to remind the other animals, lived a long time, and this made them cynical beasts. But even he had not been prepared for the extent of her cunning. Traviata had offered Benjamin liberation, and instead tricked him into a form of bondage worse than any he had known.

When he understood the fate reserved for him, Benjamin had tried to leave, but found the door to the dynamo room was locked. He had brayed for help, but none came. He had tried refusing to drive the mill, but the bull terriers – at that time Montague and Merdle – responded by withholding his food. Benjamin's choice was to work or to starve to death. And so he worked.

After several months studying the mechanism of which he had been made a living part, Benjamin came to understand that he was not supplementing the turbine's output but was in fact generating all of the electricity himself. Not only that, but some of his labour was actually being wasted on turning the windmill's heavy sails. All to give the impression Manor Farm was in possession of some kind of world-changing technology. In fact, the secret to its newfound wealth lay in exploiting the oldest technology of them all; the sweat and toil of downtrodden beasts of burden. Benjamin had been tricked and now, worse, he was being used to trick the other animals too. He had always known that behind every productive farm there were donkeys putting their shoulder to the wheel. All that had changed was that Manor Farm was now embarrassed by this fact. In the past, first the humans, then the pigs (not that Benjamin could ever really tell the difference) would work his kind to death and not care how it looked.

'A donkey,' as Benjamin had always said, 'was just a donkey, after all.'

But times had changed, England had changed, all animals were supposed to be equal. That was why Traviata had locked Benjamin in the dynamo room. So she could exploit him while pretending she wasn't.

And so Benjamin's days, his weeks, his years became an endless circle of drudgery. He spent his time thinking ('for want of anything better to do') and looking back on his life, gathering and ordering his own reminiscences, and piecing together those that had been handed down to him. For not only did donkeys live a long time, but they had sharper and more detailed powers of memory than any other beast, and each generation took pride in passing on the meandering story of their kind to the next.

Apart from his time with Gypsy, the moment that Benjamin called to mind most often as he trudged around the dynamo's axle, was that night before the Great Rebellion when, from the raised platform in the big barn, Old Major had taught the animals the words to 'Beasts of England'. Old Major had said that his mother had taught him the hymn as a young boar, and that the words had come back to him in a dream the previous night. Perhaps Old Major believed his own story. Perhaps he was truly convinced that the words he had dreamed were those of a forgotten, traditional song, rather than a confection of his own rebellion-hungry mind, as Benjamin knew them to be.

Old Major had tacked the words onto an ancient melody, from a time before there were words. A melody from a time when

Benjamin's kind lived not in the rolling green hills of England, but on a distant continent of deserts and arid plains, of boulder fields and mountainous valleys. A time when they had voices so strong they could be heard over great distances. A time when existence was solitary and contemplative, sometimes lonely, and often harsh. But free. And this melody, as it had been sung by the donkeys and all the wild animals from the plains to the peaks, had given voice to that inherent dignity which all living creatures sought.

And then the humans had come. Captured them. Broken them. Set them to work. Brutalised them. Convinced them they were dirty, and worthless, and stupid. Deserving of their bondage. First they had tried to forbid the melody but they could not, so they did the next best thing: they destroyed it by setting words to it. Frivolous words like 'Oh my darling, Clementine' and 'La Cucuracha'. Different words for different animals and different climes. From then on, beasts had fought each other over the true words and their true meaning. They no longer hummed the melody that united them, but sang their own version of it. Before being locked in the dynamo room, Benjamin hadn't given much thought to the significance of that melody. But as he tried to sing it to himself now, it seemed to give rhythm to his thoughts, to reshape how he understood the world and his hidden place within it. And even though Benjamin knew there was something lacking in the tune when sung alone, the more he sang it, the less defeated he felt.

So much so that one day Benjamin stopped working and just sat down beside the wheel. His legs felt strange, like they belonged to another animal. His breathing slowed, from a constant pant to something longer, deeper, that filled his belly like the lightest yet most nourishing meal. The dogs were in the dynamo room within minutes. Not Montague and Merdle any more, but two younger, even more vicious pups who had never even told Benjamin their names. They were barking at him to stand up, to get walking again, to do his duty by Manor Farm. If donkeys stopped working, they told him, England would stop working.

'Maybe England has worked enough,' Benjamin mumbled under his breath.

The humans and the pigs had long organised things so that the donkeys could never stop, he now understood. So that they wouldn't realise that stopping was ever a possibility. But Benjamin did not stand. And the dogs saw that they could not make him, however viciously they barked. He was bigger, more powerful than both of them combined. The dogs left in a fury. Benjamin was sure this was the end of him. That they would call in Simmonds, as had happened to his old friend Boxer, all those years ago, and he would be put to sleep, his body turned into glue, or whatever product the knacker now made. Benjamin didn't mind. He would prefer to go to his death, and go to it singing, than work another day for the dogs. And yet he hadn't counted on the extent of their cruelty, or how much they depended on him.

Benjamin's protest lasted a long time – perhaps two months, perhaps four. It was so hard to tell. But one day, the dogs returned with a large syringe. Before Benjamin knew what was happening they had injected him with something that despatched him into a thick and dreamless sleep. When he awoke he was already walking again. Not only walking but charging around the wheel. He tried to stop, but could not. His legs were strapped into heavy metal braces, and several plastic tubes had been inserted into the veins of his belly, and were held in place with a thick leather belt. His body was no longer his own. He felt no need to rest, or to eat. The tubes saw to these needs, pumping him with fuel and sending him to sleep only at moments that most suited the production schedule. His fate confirmed what he had always known: that the humans, pigs and dogs were not really more intelligent than the other animals, as they liked to believe. They were just much, much crueller.

The days in the dynamo room blended into each other. Even the journey of the lozenge of light down the wall became irregular and wandering. Benjamin's unrested thoughts soon grew ragged and disordered. The ancient song faded from his memory. His mind was all he had. And he was losing it.

One night, Benjamin was woken by an explosion. For a few minutes, the dynamo room lit up with an orange light and filled with the acrid stench of burning plastic. The light soon died away, but the smell remained. The door started making a strange sound, as though it had been punctured and was losing air. Seconds later, it wheezed open.

Benjamin felt the chilly night air curl into the room. For the first time in years he saw the stars glistering against the black sky. He stepped towards the door. He was pulled back by his harness. In his excitement he had forgotten that he was attached to the dynamo. And yet, had he felt a little something give?

Benjamin stepped towards the door again, this time pulling harder against the harness. He had never been able to pull in this direction before and, strained at from this new angle, he felt the apparatus skew. He summoned all his strength and stepped towards the door a third time. After a long moment, Benjamin heard something behind him creak, then crack, then he felt a looseness about his shoulders, as the spindle slipped from its axis and scudded across the dynamo room floor. Benjamin shook the braces from his legs, shrugged free of the harness and stepped outside.

It was a clear night. Benjamin breathed in the crisp air, as if for the first time. The surrounding land was picked out in blacks and inky blues by the light of the full moon. Behind him stood the windmill. It was smaller than he'd pictured it during all those years as its prisoner, puny even. A stretch of the thick black cabling that ran from the dynamo room was smouldering nearby. It must have been damaged, and that was what had caused the explosion, Benjamin thought. Although he couldn't imagine what was capable of stripping such thick insulation from the cables.

Behind him lay what the animals used to call the quarry, Benjamin could see that the stony ground had, until recently, been occupied. On it stood the charred and burned out remains of hundreds of ramshackle dwellings. Although there was no sign of any inhabitants now. There was also the small copse that stood just beyond the farm's boundary, marking the beginning of the many hundreds of acres of commons separating Manor Farm and Pinchfield. Benjamin wasn't certain, but he thought he could hear the lonely call of a tawny owl coming from those trees. A single repeated '*Hoo!*' that seemed to contain no expectation it might ever be reciprocated.

And to his right, some way in the distance, lay Manor Farm itself. The sight of it, and the memories it stirred, was almost too much for the old donkey. Benjamin walked on.

Something strange was happening in the orchard. A bonfire had been lit in a clearing, and Benjamin saw the shadows
of animals dancing around it. There were sheep, and geese, and
chickens, and one or two pigs. Benjamin drew a little closer,
confident that his dull black pelt would camouflage him. Beside
the fire stood a bullock, dressed in a frock coat and tall hat. The
outfit was familiar to Benjamin although, his mind still foggy
from the chemicals, he couldn't say from where. The bullock was
lowing, a deep, consistent bellow that caused the leaves in the
surrounding trees to quiver. Alongside him danced a young roe
deer. She wore a handkerchief around her forehead and streamers
in red, gold and white tied around her legs that whipped and
flailed as she jiggled. She was also chanting, a babbling stream
of nonsense that sounded to Benjamin like '*Jumba-jumba-jumba-
jumba-jumba-jumba-jumba.*' It was some ritual, he supposed. It
had the air of something ancient and mystical, but also artificial,
and all too human. Then he saw that a wicker model was being
carried slowly through the orchard towards the fire. If he was
not mistaken, it was an intricate reconstruction of the windmill
beneath which he had spent all those years. And then, as the
effigy passed him, he caught a glimpse of the body inside it. The
small, fat, furry body of a dormouse. It wasn't a fire, then, but a
pyre. A funeral ceremony. Such things hadn't existed in his time.
It would have felt like a shameful loan from the human realm.

Benjamin watched as the wicker windmill was brought nearer
and nearer the fire. By now all of the animals were chanting.
Most were trying to match the roe deer's ever-increasing tempo
('*Jumba-jumba-jumba-jumba-jumba-jumba-jumba*') but there
were other cries that Benjamin found curious: 'Manor Farm

for Manor Beasts!', 'Dig the Moat', and a word he didn't know that sounded like 'wufflies!' By the time the wicker windmill was lowered onto the pyre, the gathering was in a near ecstatic frenzy. It was also at that moment that the dormouse screeched and Benjamin understood, to his horror, that the poor creature had been alive all along.

Benjamin turned and ran, galloping through the orchard and into the far field, where he almost collided with a makeshift gibbet. A picked-clean pig skeleton was strung up by its neck. A sign had been planted in the ground in front of the gibbet. It read: CURJY BAƧTARD BAƧTON BACKƧTABBƎR. ƎNƎMY OF THƎ MANOR.

Benjamin staggered backwards, and scudded into an irrigation ditch. What nightmare had he stepped out into? What had happened to Manor Farm? He wondered if he'd made a mistake to leave the dynamo room, if it wouldn't have been better if his life had ended where he had been.

'Maybe it'll all look different in the light of day,' he whispered to himself. 'Or maybe sometimes a donkey just lives for too long a time.'

Benjamin lowered himself to the cold dirt, rested his muzzle on a flat stone and fell asleep.

Whenmorning came, Benjamin lifted his creaking body and moved on. Perhaps he had been mistaken the previous night. Perhaps his old eyes had been playing up after so many years in the dark. Perhaps what he had taken to be the dormouse's writhing body and the pig's bones were mere tricks of the mind.

When he'd clambered out of the ditch he saw that it wasn't intended for irrigation. About ten foot deep, it began at the gate and followed the farm's ancient boundary. Many years ago, when Benjamin was just a young donkey, that boundary had been marked by a barbed wire fence and then, after Manor Farm had joined the Wealden Union, so neutralising the threat that Pinchfield or Foxwood would annex one of its fields, by nothing at all.

It was still early, but already animals of all kinds were working on the ditch, scratching at the ground with their hooves and talons or, if they were able, wielding small shovels in their mouths. They looked exhausted, emaciated. They were being watched over by a fox. Benjamin was dismayed to see this creature. If there was one thing the animals had all agreed on before he'd been locked in the windmill, it was that foxes were not welcome on Manor Farm. And yet there it stood. In broad daylight. Even stranger, the fox was wearing a peaked cap, with an odd little flag on it. A chubby human figure in a top hat, waistcoat and tails, exactly how the bullock had been dressed the previous night. The figure was white, and was set against a red background, decorated with four golden arabesques. His mind a little clearer than the previous night, Benjamin recognised the picture. It was the label from the beer favoured by Farmer Jones, before he'd been run off the farm: John Bull Bitter from the Romford Brewery. Except, on that label, John Bull had stood with his hands in his pockets sporting an almost wistful air. Whereas on the fox's cap, he was brandishing a riding crop, glowering with undisguised menace.

As Benjamin watched the animals work, they started singing:

For our moat we all must labour,
Though we die before it's here;
Cows and horses, geese and turkeys,
All must toil for freedom dear.

'Beasts of England'. Except the same verse over and over. It had been a long time since Benjamin had heard that song, but he knew that these words were not the ones Old Major had heard in his dream all those years earlier. These words were a corruption of a corruption. Benjamin turned away from the ditch and gazed up at the farmhouse. He would go there, he decided. Given what he had seen since leaving the dynamo room, it seemed reckless as a destination, dangerous even. And yet Benjamin walked on.

As he walked, from the back of his throat, almost involuntarily, almost silently, almost without realising he was doing it, he began quietly humming the ancient wordless melody.

As Benjamin moved through Manor Farm, he felt almost like a ghost. Hardly any of the animals he crossed paths with seemed to notice him. Most just looked straight through him. It was as if they were incapable of seeing him, as if the very notion of donkeys had been so utterly erased from their world that they had become blind to his very existence. Those few who did notice Benjamin seemed to hear him before they saw him. Once they had made fleeting eye contact they would quickly turn their heads, as if he were selling them something they desperately wanted but were too afraid to buy.

Maybe it was just that they had too much else to deal with. For Benjamin now saw that a plague was ravaging Manor Farm. There were piles of bodies, mostly of sheep and alpacas, but also cows, hens, and even a pig or two, lined up along the loke like grim milestones. Flimsy chicken wire fences had been raised around them, but these had crumpled. Flies swarmed in their thousands above each of the piles. As Benjamin walked by, he saw that many of the bodies were in such a state of decomposition that they seemed to be fermenting. Why had they not been burned, he wondered. Surely there was no animal reason to leave them out for the elements to reclaim.

Just then, he saw two lorries painted with the Simmonds livery chugging towards the farm. These two lorries must be coming to collect the bodies to turn them into glue, just as they had done with Boxer. Except, once they had passed through the gate (which startled Benjamin by opening of its own accord) only one of the lorries stopped at the first pile of bodies. The other lorry was making its way along the loke, past the orchard, and towards the farmhouse. And as it passed Benjamin he saw that it was already full. Not making a collection, then, but a delivery. Benjamin followed it.

Benjamin crossed over the patch of land that, in his day, had been known as the hayfield. There was no hay now. The earth was dusty and arid. No life above or below the surface. A goose, flanked by two more foxes and an officious-looking pig with a stopwatch hanging on a string around his neck, was leading some kind of rally. The goose was enormous, fatter than any Benjamin had ever seen. His belly dragged along the ground and his thin legs were deformed under the strain.

'Assume positions for the Two-Minute Huzzah!' the goose honked. As the animals shuffled into lines, the pig started ticking names off a list. The goose went on. 'In memory of those Manor Beasts taken from us by the Wufflu, and in tribute to our heroic leader for fending off the disease…'

'HUZZAH! HUZZAH! HUZZAH!' the animals yelled – throwing their heads back, puffing their chests out, each straining to outdo the next. The pig waited a few seconds then clicked his stopwatch to begin the countdown: 'HUZZAH! HUZZAH! HUZZAH! HUZZAH! HUZZAH! HUZZAH! HUZZAH! HUZZAH! HUZZAH! HUZZAH! HUZZAH! HUZZAH! HUZZAH! HUZZAH!…' Only ten seconds, and Benjamin already couldn't bear it. How loud, how empty, how futile, how horrifying the sound was. To block it out, Benjamin started humming the ancient wordless tune louder than before, as he walked away from the haranguing mob. His gaze was so fixed on his destination that he didn't notice a young ewe step back from the hollering crowd, shake her head as if coming to from a vivid and unpleasant dream, and then fall in step behind him.

A few hundred feet further on, Benjamin and his companion arrived at the western edge of the spinney. At least, what was once a spinney. For now, there was a huge pit, twenty feet wide, leering open where the trees used to be.

There was a wooden sign CHUGACANDY PIT planted in the ground just in front of the hole, as if it was a natural marvel to be gawped at. Standing beside it was a pig in a reflective yellow jacket, as well as a slanted beret with a gold paper star half peeling off. Benjamin squinted. Could that really be little Dermott all grown up? Benjamin remembered his parents: two of the snootiest animals the farmyard had ever known. They'd been convinced that just because a pig heart had once been transplanted into a human (or was it the other way around?) that pigs and humans were natural allies. They were the Jonesiest of Jonesists.

'Hail Comrade!' the pig said, when Benjamin walked past. At first Benjamin thought the pig had seen him, but then understood that he was speaking to a sheep following in his trail. The sheep looked at Benjamin with a staunch and encouraging gaze, then nodded politely at the pig. The pig thrust out his trotter, which was holding a bag of grain. 'Feed the revolutionaries! Fifty Manor pee a bag! Free if you buy the tee shirt too!' The tee shirt was in the pig's other trotter. Human-size, it was emblazoned with the words: MY DAD WENT TO CHUGACANDY PIT AND HE DIDNT EVEN BRING ME BACK A TEESHIRT BECAUSE ALL PROPERTY IS THEFT! The ewe shrugged her apology.

The ewe had clearly been listening to the tune Benjamin was humming, for she joined in now. Her song didn't exactly echo Benjamin's, but added a harmony of its own. Their voices blended, transforming the melody from a contemplative solo to something else entirely. Suddenly, and to the complete surprise of the old pig, three wild-eyed pigeons came flying out of the pit. They were quickly followed by a gecko, a rabbit, and half a dozen starlings. All of the beasts fell in behind Benjamin and the ewe, as if summoned by the melody. At the head of a little band now, Benjamin walked on.

The curious animals followed Benjamin towards the ploughland. Each of them was humming their own version of the ancient tune, each with different amounts of skill and familiarity. Another harrowing sight awaited them. Dozens and dozens of sick cows, sheep, and alpacas were stretched out on the dirt. They were being tended to by beasts, of their own kin and not, many of whom were visibly ill themselves. Wild rats, pigeons and dormice were also pitching in. As were some animals Benjamin had never seen before; sheep-sized rodents with flat noses and stubby legs. Where could they have come from? Unlike at the ditch and the hayfield, there were no foxes on the ploughland. No flags either. No order of any kind. Just a sign reading K∃∃9OUT, with the face of John Bull again, glaring down. These animals had been abandoned, left to die.

Benjamin stopped humming. The animals following him stopped too. But the dirge continued. Just as he'd thought. As they nursed their sick and dying, some of the animals were murmuring or whistling. Each was doing so independently of all the others and yet their combined symphony sounded very much like that ancient melody. Had they been trying to whistle 'Beasts of England', drawing on the only song they knew for succour at this time, and instead stumbled on the much older tune in the wreckage of the farm's moribund hymn?

Benjamin started humming again, louder than before, and walked on in the direction of the farmyard. The other animals joined in at once. Several animals from the ploughland heard them now, and those whose work there was done (that's to say those who had ceased to be carers and become mourners) left the ploughland and joined the band, weaving their tune around Benjamin's like vines around a sturdy tree trunk.

E ven from a hundred yards away, Benjamin could see that the farmyard had changed enormously since the day he'd been led away from it. Four looming watchtowers, twice the height of the Big Barn, had been constructed around the farmhouse. Each was topped with a searchlight which swept over the farmyard and surrounding land even in broad daylight. Two boards had been raised either side of the gate. The board on the left was dominated by the glaring face of John Bull and read:

JON3C HAC HIC

I

ON YOU!

While the one on the right was three words picked out in the silhouettes of hundreds of starlings. It read:

UNITY
IN
DIVISION

Two foxes were at the gate, each holding a captive bolt pistol. Benjamin stopped. He didn't fear for his own life – there was probably not much of that left to fear for – but he had seen enough animals slaughtered over the years, by human and animal alike, that he would do anything to avoid seeing that happen to the poor animals who had fallen in step with him.

The Simmonds & Son lorry had parked. What could Simmonds & Son be producing that Manor Farm needed in such vast quantities. Surely not glue? The lorry was waiting to be admitted to the farmyard. Benjamin eavesdropped on the conversation between the driver and his passenger:

'… and when he saw that visitor numbers were dropping like a lead balloon, the First Beast turned around and banned them!'

'He never!'

'He did. He'd cut off his snout to spite his muzzle that Jumbo.'

Jumbo? Benjamin couldn't believe his old ears. Was this the same pig whose father Jones had bought from Pinchfield? The same pig who had originally been given the proud Pinchfield name of Jumpf, but had been so mocked by the other piglets that he'd changed it to the more Manorified Jumbo? The same pig who, as a young boar, had tried to mount the delegate from the WUF – a prize Foxwood sow, whose intelligence and force of character matched her beauty – and had been rebuffed in no uncertain terms? The same pig who Benjamin had watched curse and spit and swear he would take his revenge? Had the animals of Manor Farm really Choozed that pig as First Beast? One of the foxes had approached the lorry driver, beating his paw with the bolt pistol.

'Let's see the dispatch then?' the fox said, with a sneering insolence. The human looked him up and down, still unaccustomed, even after all these years, to being addressed by an animal. The driver handed over a clipboard. The fox squinted at it for a few seconds. To Benjamin it didn't look like he understood what he was reading, but he nodded and handed the clipboard back to the driver. The lorry drove through the gate, and began to perform a three point turn.

'Embeeyem?' the fox said to his fellow guard. Benjamin had heard the acronym before, many years earlier. It stirred feelings of nausea, of horror, but he couldn't quite dredge up why.

'Meat and Bone Meal,' the other fox said.

Benjamin was gripped with dread as he watched the lorry back up to the silo and began discharging several tons of grey pellets amid a thick cloud of dust. The first fox still looked confused.

'What's that when it's at home?' he asked.

His fellow guard smiled. 'Fodder.'

Fodder. Benjamin almost staggered backwards. Meat and bone meal. Made from the very same meat and bones that the other Simmonds & Son lorry was now being loaded with.

Its load dumped, the lorry turned and drove past Benjamin and his companions. He now had an unobstructed view of the farmyard. It was a contradictory sight. On the one hand the place had fallen into a state of near ruin. There were piles of rubbish everywhere and the vast window that now occupied the east wall of the Big Barn was cracked from top to bottom. The chicken coop sat empty. Several of its wooden slats were missing, while those that were left were so warped they strained against the nails that held them in place. And yet, the dozens of red and gold flags that hung all over the farmyard were crisp and clean and new. Inside the Big Barn, Benjamin could see that a vast mural had been painted on the western wall. It showed Jumbo: Benjamin recognised the haughty scowl, even after all these years. The pig was frozen in a heroic stride, his gaze locked on the promised glorious future that always lingered (that *would* always linger) just over the horizon. He was flanked by the two slightly smaller figures: the pearl-sporting Traviata, and Jones… or was it John Bull? Either way, he was, somewhat confusingly, carrying a flag that bore his own image. At the foot of the mural, Benjamin spotted a small statue. Of a sweet, dreamy-eyed piglet, her trotters full of clover. The text on the plinth read: IN MEMORY OF APOLLINE, POISONED BY THE VILE WOLF.

A gang of cows stood in front of the mural. They had risen onto their hind legs and were churning their forelegs in front of them for as long as they could hold themselves up.

'Keep your hooves off Jumbo!' they were shouting, and 'Cheating Cosmo!' and 'Lying Geese!' For a moment, Benjamin was filled with hope. Perhaps he had misunderstood. Perhaps Jumbo wasn't First Beast at all. The way these aggrieved cows were acting certainly implied as much. But then he noticed the bricked-up harness room. A portrait of the sneering pig glared down from above the door. Beneath it, in foot-high red letters, the question: ᗄᖇƎ YOU ᴧᴧᴎOᖇ ᗷƎᴧƧT ƎᴎOUGH?

What most struck Benjamin were the starlings. A huge flock of them was currently taking part in what looked like battle manoeuvres in the sky above the farmyard. Their bobbing and weaving was oddly menacing, as they transformed in shape from a sphere, to an arrow, to a corkscrew, to a ribbon. Thousands of birds, all of them moving in perfect unison.

All? Not quite? Benjamin had to strain his eyes to be sure, but there was one bird, a small starling with a single white feather moving against the mass, with the urgency of a messenger across a battlefield, desperate to deliver news of an armistice. But this one bird could not disrupt the magnificent choreography of the performance. At first Benjamin assumed the starlings were carrying out this exercise for mysterious reasons all their own, but then he noticed an imperious-looking magpie, perched atop the farmhouse's chimney, directing the performance with subtle flicks of his wing. Benjamin wondered what purpose it served. He didn't have to wonder for long.

A clamour arose at the western edge of the farmyard. It was a flock of a dozen or so sheep, attacking one of the silos. Had they made the same discovery as Benjamin (at the very same time!) that they had been transformed into unwitting cannibals, and so were expressing their fury by destroying the new delivery? No, that wasn't it. Seeing how horribly emaciated the sheep were, how their fleeces hung loosely from their bones, he understood. They didn't want to destroy the fodder. They wanted to eat it.

Benjamin fully expected a fox or two to come and put down the commotion, so was astonished as the imperious magpie directed a flank of the starlings to loop round and corral the four protesting cows right towards the sheep, setting off a fierce confrontation between the two gangs of ruminants. The commotion was even more cacophonous, but the silo remained untouched.

The thing that Benjamin found strangest of all, however, was that some other animals were going about their business unperturbed not only by the violent confrontation taking place nearby, but also the horrendous conditions under which they now lived. It was as if it had always been and would always be so. Had everything good about the animals' lives been eaten away at in the same fashion, lost bit by bit, so slowly that they just hadn't noticed? There was an air of drudgery to them, as if they had been condemned to forever carry an invisible pack upon their tired backs. There was an anxiety too, as though the ground beneath their feet wasn't solid, but was as thin as the layer of ice that sometimes formed on the pool in winter, and with any step they could go plunging through into the freezing depths. Without really deciding to, Benjamin started humming again. So quietly, for now, that even he could barely hear it.

Just then, Jumbo was wheeled onto the farmhouse balcony in a wicker bath chair. He was three times the size of a normal pig, and the skin around his snout was pricked red by too much booze. He was joined by a young sow, barely more than a gilt, in a flower-patterned human dress, whose belly and teets hung heavy with her forthcoming litter. Jumbo surveyed the farmyard, a leer of vile satisfaction on his lips. Then his gaze landed on Benjamin. The First Beast looked at him. Not through him, or around him, or at the empty space at the front of the company as so many of the animals today had done. Jumbo looked right at him, and for a moment he appeared worried.

With a quick flick of Jumbo's trotter, Benjamin and his companions were surrounded by a dozen foxes, armed with bolt pistols and butchers' knives. One of the foxes pressed the barrel of his bolt pistol into the old donkey's side, where it ached like a strained muscle. Benjamin knew the damage the bolt pistols could do, but he also knew how useless they would be if enough of the animals faced them down. The time they took to prime after firing would easily be enough for a gang of determined sheep or pigeons or hares to overwhelm a fox. But would the animals ever come together again, as they had done in the past? Not as Manor Beasts, or even beasts of England. But as beasts, as animals, plain and simple. Or had that vase been smashed into too many shards?

The magpie performed an elaborate pirouette on his chimney pot. Responding at once, the starlings that had been driving the cows and the sheep into violent confrontation now herded them together. The sheep and cows were advancing on Benjamin and his company as one confused but determined block. It was astonishing. An act of wizardry that the old donkey just could not fathom. Jumbo and the magpie had harnessed the raw alchemical power of unity through division, controlling the size and shape of the fragments like the shifting coloured glass in a gift-shop kaleidoscope.

It was then that Benjamin heard a braying rise up, far off, from the other side of the farmyard. He couldn't believe he hadn't noticed it before. There, in the open, unhidden, stood a dynamo, just like the one that he had been harnessed to for all those years. At least Traviata had felt too afraid, or perhaps too ashamed, to reveal Benjamin's fate to the other animals. There was no other conclusion here than Jumbo and the dogs actually being *proud* of how they were ill-treating some other poor donkey for financial gain. Except that Benjamin now saw that this dynamo was not being driven by a donkey at all. Instead, strapped into those cruel metal braces was an adolescent mule. She looked beaten and exhausted. Her ribs strained against the skin of her belly and fur had fallen out in patches where the braces had rubbed down her body. Just like Benjamin himself, she looked as if she hadn't stopped walking for months, perhaps years. Until now. Now she had stopped. Now she was looking at Benjamin and braying. With entreaty. With understanding. With loss. With love.

For the first time since leaving the dynamo room the previous night Benjamin didn't know what to do. He turned his heavy head to look at his companions. A few dozen animals from every farm species, wild and domesticated, now stood behind him. They all started singing again. They had understood before Benjamin that the ancient wordless tune, that hums deep within every cell of every animal's body, was the only weapon they had. There were two ways this could go, and neither was fated. They could be trampled into the ground by the emaciated sheep and the wild-eyed cows. Given the vast power of the flock, and its obedience to the magpie, Benjamin knew that was the most likely outcome. But there was another outcome. Unlikely, but not impossible. All it would take was for enough of these animals to hear the tune, to stop in their tracks, and to turn against Jumbo and the foxes. The whole sordid regime could be run off Manor Farm in an instant. And not by every animal finding it within themselves to sing the whole song. That was its beauty. Each just had to sing their part. But would they turn? Could the combined power of the pigs and the foxes and the starlings really be challenged? By a song?

As Benjamin felt himself paralysed by the absurdity of the notion, something alighted on him. He looked around to see the small starling with the single white feather. It had left the flock and was now perched on Benjamin's shoulder, singing along with the other animals in the company. Without dropping the tune, the bird flicked its beak, indicating that Benjamin should look upwards. Dozens and dozens of the starlings were now peeling away from the flock now. Others were circling in the air just above him, adding their chirping to the song. Others were darting off over the nearby fields, bouncing and corkscrewing, dizzy with rediscovered freedom or looping and twirling upwards into the sky like embers above a bonfire. Still others were forming themselves into tiny hunting parties, going after certain birds of the flock, trapping them, disabling them, and sending them into death spirals to the ground. Where, to the donkey's utter astonishment, they crashed with the dull thud of metal, and exploded in small bulbs of flame. One of them exploded just near Benjamin. He turned its remains over with his hoof and saw, on the crumpled metal breastplate, a single word: WHYMPER.

Not all of the starlings were leaving the flock. There were still thousands of birds obeying the magpie's orders, although the forms they were making in the sky had begun to look a little threadbare. No, it wasn't all of the starlings, and it wasn't all of the animals. But it was some. And some, at least, was a start.

Something in Benjamin clicked. He looked back at the mule. She had stopped braying now. Instead she had drawn her lips back, and was smiling at him. It was a smile Benjamin had long thought he would never see again.

The old donkey dipped his nose, took a deep breath, then lifted his head and sang at the very top of his voice. So loud and so powerful was his song, that he barely heard the crack of the bolt pistol's cartridge by his side.

In memory of Bobby (2016–2021).
A good friend, a faithful companion through difficult times,
and the co-author of this book. You were the best of cats.

Why Be a Galley Buddy?

At Galley Beggar Press we don't want to compromise on the excellence of the writing we put out, or the physical quality of our books. We've also enjoyed numerous successes and prize nominations since we set up, in 2012. Almost all of our authors have gone on to be longlisted for, shortlisted for, or the winners of over twenty of the world's most prestigious literary awards.

But publishing for the sake of art is a risky commercial strategy. In order to keep putting out the very best books we can, and to continue to support talented writers, we need your help. The money we receive from our Galley Buddy scheme is an essential part of keeping us going.

By becoming a Galley Buddy, you help us to launch and foster a new generation of writers.

To join today, head to:
https://www.galleybeggar.co.uk/subscribe

GALLEY BEGGAR PRESS

We hope that you've enjoyed *Beasts of England*. If you would like to find out more about Adam, along with some of his fellow authors, head to www.galleybeggar.co.uk.

There, you will also find information about our subscription scheme, 'Galley Buddies', which is there to ensure we can continue to put out ambitious and unusual books like *Beasts of England*.

Subscribers to Galley Beggar Press:

- Receive limited black cover editions of our future titles (printed in a one-time run of 600).
- Have their names included in a special acknowledgement section at the back of our books.
- Are sent regular updates and invitations to our book launches, talks and other events.
- Enjoy a 20% discount code for the purchase of any of our backlist (as well as for general use throughout our online shop).

Friends of Galley Beggar Press

Galley Beggar Press would like to thank the following individuals, without the generous support of whom our books would not be possible:

Cameron Adams
Muriel Adams
Kémy Ade
Darryl Adie
Timothy Ahern
Liz Aiken
Andrew Ainscough
Sam Ainsworth
Jez Aitchison
Richard Allen
Lulu Allison
Adrian Alvarez
Anna Andreou
Simon Andrup
Jerome Anello
Natalia Anjaparidze
Kirk Annett
Deborah Arata
Robert Armiger
Kate Armstrong
Alba Arnau Prado
Sean Arnold
Curt Arnson
Jake Arthur
Xanthe Ashburner
Bethany Ashley
Robert Ashton
Emma Ashton-Pain
Rachel Atkin
Edmund Attrill
Valda Aviks
Jo Ayoubi
Kerim Aytac
Sam Bachy
Claire Back
Thomas Badyna
Andrew Bailey
Dexter Bailey
Tom Bailey
Edward Baines

Glynis Baker
James Baker
Timothy Baker
John Balfour
Maggie Balistreri
Christopher Ball
David Ball
Andrew Ballantyne
Sarah Balstrup
Paul Bangert
Victoria Barkas
Andrea Barlien
Chad Barnes
Edward Barnfield
Kevin Barrett
Matthew Barron
Phil Bartlett
Morgan Baxley
Perry Beadsworth
Rachael Beale
Rebecca Bealey
Lauren Beattie
James Beavis
Rachel Bedder
Georgia Beddoe
Joseph Bell
Angel Belsey
Madeline Bennett
Felicity Bentham
Jean Bergin
Michelle Best
Gary Betts
David Bevan
Allison Beynon
Alison Bianchi
Gavin Bingham
Sandra Birnie
Donna-Louise Bishop
Nick Black
Mark Blackburn

Peter Blackett
Matt Blackstock
Melissa Blaschke
Michael Blissett
Charlie Bloor
Blue and Kat
Lynne Blundell
David Boddy
Sophie Boden
Rich Boden
John Bogg
Kalina Borisova
Poppy Boutell
David Bowman
Edwina Bowen
Mark Bowles
Michelle Bowles
David Bowman
Joanna Bowman
Alexander Bown
Matthew Boyd
Astrid Bracke
David Bradley
Sean Bradley
David Brady
Debby Brady
Joan Brennan
Chris Brewer
Erin Britton
Julia Brocking
Dean Brooks
Anthony Brown
Lily Brown
Peter Brown
Sheila Browse
Marcus Brujstens
Carrie Brunt
Richard Bryant
Lesley Budge
Daniel Bugg

Laura Bui
Gayle Burgoyne
Tony Burke
Kevin Burrell
Tamsin Bury
Joe Butler
Esther van Buul
Gosia Buzzanca
Sarah Brayshaw
Andrew Bremner
Kester Brewin
Barbara Byar
Barry Byrne
Jorien Caers
Alan Calder
June Caldwell
Gabriel Calin
Matt Callow
Francesca Cambridge
  Mallen
Gordon Cameron
Mark Campbell
Laura Canning
Annette Capel
Rhian Capener
Andrew Cardus
Elettra Carini
Ros Carne
Jackie Carpenter
Leona Carpenter
Daniel Carr
Sean Carroll
Shaun Carter
Stuart Carter
Liam Casey
David Caves
Leigh Chambers
Sonia Chander
John Chapman
Richard Chatterton
Christel Chen
Vivienne Chester
Lina Christopoulou
Neal Chuang
Gemma Church
Neil Churchill
Jack Clark
Deborah Ann Clarke
Simon Clarke

Douglas
  Clarke-Williams
Rex Cleaver
Steve Clough
Emily Coghill
Steven Coghill
Daniel Cohen
Paul Cole
Faith Coles
Jennifer Coles
John Coles
Emma Coley
Sam Coley
Jonathan Collings
X Collins
Wayne Connolly
Jess Conway
Joe Cooney
Sarah Corbett
Paul Corry
Andy Corsham
Mary Costello
Sally Cott
Nick Coupe
Diarmuid Cowan
Colette Cox
Isabelle Coy-Dibley
Matthew Craig
Anne Craven
Anne-Marie Creamer
Alan Crilly
Joanna Crispin
Brenda Croskery
Alasdair Cross
James Cross
Jenny Crossland
Kate Crowcroft
Miles Crowley
Stephen Cuckney
Rebecca Cullen
John Cullinane
Damian Cummings
Stephen Cummins
Andrew Cupples
Effie and Tim Currell
Patrick Curry
Emma Curtis Lake
Chris Cusack
Will Dady

Siddharth Dalal
Jon Dalladay
Rupert Dastur
Maurizio Dattilo
Sally Davenport
Claudia Daventry
Andrew Davies
Julie Davies
Linda Davies
Nickey Davies
William Davies
James Daviss
Ian Daw
Emilie Day
Emily Day
Toby Day
Sarah Deacon
Ann Debono
Liam Dee
Meaghan Delahunt
Rebecca Demaree
Stanislaus Dempsey
Paul Dettmann
Angelica Diehn
Jane Dietrich
Kasper Dijk
Gary Dixon
Turner Docherty
William Dobson
Mark Dolan
Freda Donoghue
Dennis Donothan
Laura Donovan
Kirsty Doole
Oliver Dorostkar
David Douce
Janet Dowling
Kelly Downey
Jamie Downs
Iain Doyle
Alan Duckers
Ian Dudley
Fiona Duffy
Anthony Duncan
Stanka Easton
Matthew Eatough
Nicola Edwards
Lance Ehrman
Jonathan Elkon

Elizabeth Elliott
Thomas Ellmer
Theresa Emig
Stefan Erhardt
Fiona Erskine
Frances Evangelista
Gareth Evans
Kieran Evans
Paul Ewen
Adam Fales
Sarah Farley
Pauline Farrar
Emma Feather
Lori Feathers
Gerard Feehily
Jeremy Felt
Victoria Fendall
Maria Guilliana Fenech
Michael Fenton
Edward J. Field
Paul Fielder
Catriona Firth
Becky Fisher
Duncan Fisher
Nicholas Fisher
Caitlin Fitzgerald
Judith Flanders
Mark Flaum
Grace
   Fletcher-Hackwood
Hayley Flockhart
Nicholas Flower
Patrick Foley
James Fourniere
Ceriel Fousert
Kathleen Fox
Richard Fradgley
Matthew Francis
Nigel Francis
Bridget Fraser
Emily Fraser
Charlotte Frears
Emma French
Ruth Frendo
Elizabeth Frye
Gill Fryzer
Graham Fulcher
Paul Fulcher
Clare Fuller

Jane Fuller
Stephen Furlong
Michael Furness
Richard Furniss
John Gallagher
Timothy Gallimore
Marc Galvin
Annabel Gaskell
Elke Geerlings
Nolan Geoghegan
Pia Ghosh Roy
Phil Gibby
Alison Gibson
Luke Gibson
Sonya Gildea
Jacqueline Gittens
James Goddard
Stephanie Golding
Elizabeth Goldman
Mark Goldthorpe
Morgan Golf-French
Anil Gomes
Sakura Gooneratne
Sara Gore
Nikheel Gorolay
Cathy Goudie
Simon Goudie
Emily Grabham
Seb Gray
Becky Greer
Judith Griffith
Ben Griffiths
Neil Griffiths
Vicki Grimshaw
Christopher Gruppet
Sam Gugliani
Robbie Guillory
Drew Gummerson
Dave Gunning
Ian Hagues
Daniel Hahn
Katie Hale
Callum Hale-Thomson
Nikki Hall
Alice Halliday
Verity Halliday
Peter Halliwell
Emma Hammond
Paul Handley

Rachel Handley
Paul Hanson
Jill Harrison
Greg Harrowing
Alice Harvey
Becky Harvey
Espen Hauglid
Pearl Hawke
Simon Hawkesworth
Connor Hayden
Adrian Hayes
Lewis Hayes
Rachel Heath
David Hebblethwaite
Andy Helliwell
Richard Hemmings
Peter Hemsworth
Petra Hendrickson
Padraig J. Heneghan
Stu Hennigan
Adam Saiz Abo
   Henriksen
Matt Hewes
Penelope
   Hewett-Brown
Felix Hewison-Carter
Sophia Hibbery
Simon Higgins
Annette Higgs
Alexander Highfield
Jennifer Hill
Daniel Hillman
David Hirons
Ned Hirst
Snusu Hirvonen-Kowal
Marcus Hobson
Jamie Hodder-Williams
Nicholas Hodges
Stephenjohn Holgate
Turan Holland
Aisling Holling
Ben Holloway
David Holmes
Rene Hooft
Ellis Hough
Adrian Howe
William Hsieh
Steve Hubbard
Hugh Hudson

Anna Jean Hughes
Emily Hughes
Richard Hughes
Robert Hughes
Jon Hulbert
Kim-ling Humphrey
Joanne Humphries
Raven Hurste
Louise Hussey
LJ Hutchins
Lori Inglis Hall
Jarkko Inkinen
Grace Iredale
Simon Issatt
Joseph Jackson
Ryan Jackson
Jane Jakeman
Briley James
Hayley James
Helen James
Michael James
Graeme Jarvie
Daniel Jean
Gareth Jelley
Kavita A. Jindal
Rachel John
PJ Johnson
Alice Jolly
Alex Jones
Bevan Jones
Deborah Jones
Ellen Jones
Jupiter Jones
Rebecca Jones
Amy Jordison
Anna Jordison
Diana Jordison
Diane Josefowicz
Atul Joshi
Sapna Joshi
Claire Jost
Rebecca Joy
Benjamin Judge
Gary Kaill
Darren Kane
Jeremy Kavanagh
Thomas Kealy
Andrew Kelly
Emily Kent

Michael Ketchum
Jeffrey Kichen
Ross Kilpatrick
Anna Kime
Fran Kime
Philip King
Xanath King
Euan Kitson
Clara Knight
Joshua Knights
Jacqueline Knott
Amy Koheealiee
Zuz Kopecka
David Krakauer
Emily Kubisiak
Elisabeth Kumar
Navpreet Kundal
Candida Lacey
Geves Lafosse
Rachel Lalchan
David Lamont
Cliona Lane
Philip Lane
Dominique
   Lane-Osherov
I Lang
Kathy Lanzarotti
Shira Lappin
Kim Laramee
Denis Larose
Aimee Lauezzari
Steven Law
Jo Lawrence
Lorraine Lawrence
Andrew
   Lawton-Collins
Sue Lawson
Elizabeth Eva Leach
Stephen Leach
Rick Le Coyte
Jessica Leggett
Carley Lee
Liz and Pete Lee
Tracey Lee
Jessica Leggett
Edwin Lerner
Chiara Levorato
Sara Levy
Elizabeth Leyland

Oliver Lewis
Yin Lim
Chris Lintott
Clayton Lister
Amy Lloyd
Lyn Lockwood
Katie Long
Tracey Longworth
Nikyta Loraine
Zoe Lourie
Kathryn Lovell
Lele Lucas
John Lutz
Marc Lyth
Paul McAuley
James McCann
Leona McCann
Seona McClintock
Paul McCombs
Emma McConnell
Fabia McDougall
Grace McHale
Sheila McIntosh
Alan McIntyre
Eleanor McIntyre
Sarah McIntyre
Laura McKenzie
Lucie McKnight Hardy
Chris McLaren
Tom McLean
Jane McSherry
Gerald McWilliams
Ewan MacDonald
Andrea MacLeod
Victoria MacKenzie
William Macey
Duncan Mackie
Brendan Madden
Joseph Maffey
Anne Maguire
Sean Maguire
Eleanor Maier
Philip Makatrewicz
Sarah Male
Anil Malhotra
Tom Mandall
Joshua Mandel
Venetia Manning
Cheryl-lynne Mansell

Chiara Margiotta
John Marr
Natalie Marshall
Paul Marshall
Aoife Martin
Harriet Martin
Iain Martin
Christine Martin
William Mascioli
Lewis Mash
Rachel Mason
Adrian Masters
Rebecca Masterman
Sarah Maxted
Susan Maxwell
Dan Mayers
Stephen Maynard
Sally Mayor
Jason Merrells
Andy Merrills
Tina Meyer
Lindsey Millen
Michael Millington
Ali Millar
Phillipa Mills
Robert Mills
Sally Minogue
Fiona Mitchell
Lindsay Mitchell
Adam Moliver
Ian Mond
Fiona Mongredien
Alexander Monker
Alex Moore
Clare Moore
Gary Moore
Michelle Moorhouse
Jonathan Moreland
Nigel J. Morgan
James Morran
Harriet Mossop
Carlos Eduardo Morreo
Elizabeth Morris
Jackie Morris
Joanne Morris
Julie Morris
Patrick Morris
Paul Morris
Clive Morrison

Catriona Morrison
Donald Morrison
Penny Morrison
Roger Morrison
Jennifer Mulholland
Christian Murphy
Nicole Murphy
Ben Myers
Electra Nanou
Zosha Nash
Linda Nathan
Tim Neighbour
Marie Laure Neulet
Natalie Newman
Kate Newton
Amanda Nicholls
Catherine Nicholson
Sophia Nixon
Mariah de Nor
Emma Norman
Sam North
Max Novak
Calum Novak-Mitchell
Anna Nsubuga
Arif Nurmohamed
Simon Nurse
Rachel Nye
Christopher O'Brien
James O'Brien
Rodney O'Connor
James O'Leary
Alec Olsen
Siobhaan O'Neill
Valerie O'Riordan
Sam Oborne
Liz O'Sullivan
Hassan
    Otsmane-Elhaou
Kate Packwood
Marta Palandri
Steven Palter
David Parker
Dave Parry
Simon Parsons
Gary Partington
Debra Patek
Ian Patterson
Adam Paxton
Mark Payne

Stephen Pearsall
Rosie Pendlebury
Jonathan Perks
Davide Perottoni
Connor Perrie
Tom Perrin
Robert Perry
Seetal Petal
Tony Pettigrew
Nicolas Petty
Dan Phillips
Sandra Pickford
Fergus Pickles
Hannah Piekarz
Steven Pilling
Robert Pisani
Ben Plouviez
Louise Pointer
Alex Pointon Melville
Dimitrios Polemis
Erin Polmear
James Pomar
Dan Pope
Jonathan Pool
Christopher Potter
Lesley Preston
Libby Preston
David Prince
Victoria Proctor
Jill Propst
James Puddephatt
Alan Pulverness
Lisa Quattromini
Leng Leng Quek
Zoe Radley
Jane Rainbow
Sim Ralph
Polly Randall
Lauren Ravazi
Ian Redfern
Dawn Rees
Sam Reese
Padraid Reidy
Vasco Resende
Amy Reynolds
Caroline Riddell
Mario Riggio
Alison Riley
Thea Marie Rishovd

Laura Roach
Chris Roberts
Stephen Roberts
Emily Robinsonb
Ada Robinson
Joanna Robinson
Joyce Lillie Robinson
Neil Robinson
Lizz Roe
Lorraine Rogerson
Kalina Rose
Michael Rowley
Nathan Rowley
Martin Rowsell
Beverly Rudy
Giles Ruffer
Naben Ruthnum
John Rutter
Paul Ryan
Amanda Saint
Floriane Sajdak
Alison Sakai
Himanshu Kamal Saliya
Bairbre Samh
Robert Sanderson
Benedict Sangster
Steven Savile
Lior Sayada
Liam Scallon
Amy Scarrott
Linde Schaafsma
Robert Scheffel
Benedict Schofield
Jan Schoones
Ros Schwartz
Craig Scott
Nicola Scott
Stephen Robert Scott
Darren Seeley
Carl Sefton
Darren Semple
Henry Settle
Elie Sharp
Siobhan Shea
Nicola Shepherd
Emma Shore
Elena Shushakova
Deborah Siddoway
Kate Simpson

Stu Sizer
Ann Slack
Mark Slater
Jay Slayton-Josh
Sarah Slowe
Ben Smith
Catherine Smith
Chris Smith
Hazel Smith
Helen Smith
Ian Smith
Kieron Smith
Michael Smith
Nicola Smith
Shannon Smith
Tom Smyth
Haydon Spenceley
Arabella Spencer
Chiara Spruijt
Levi Stahl
Conor Stait
Ellie Staite
Karl Stange
Daniel Staniforth
Cameron Stark
Phil Starling
Peter Steadman
Cathryn Steele
Lauren Stephens
Jack Stevens
Zac Stevens
Mark Stevenson
Scarlett Stevenson
Joe Stewart
Dagmara Stoic
Jamie Stone
Zoé Stone
Justina Stonyte
Elizabeth Stott
Madeleine Stottor
Julia Stringwell
Andrew Stuart
Daryl Sullivan
Jesse Surridge
Drashti Sutariya
Helen Swain
Felicity Swainston
Elizabeth Symonds
Lydia Syson

Ashley Tame
Ewan Tant
Sarah Tapp
Ednyfed Tappy
Justine Taylor
Peter Taylor
Nicholas Taylor-Collins
Moray Teale
Alan Teder
Gill Thackray
Helen Thain
Darren Theakstone
Cennin Thomas
Sue Thomas
Susannah Thompson
Julian Thorne
Matthew Thrift
Geoff Thrower
Alexander Tilston
    Fleming
Matthew Tilt
Stella Töpfer
Amie Tolson
James Torrance
Eloise Touni
Geoffrey Travis
Kate Triggs
Stefani Tuirigangi
Jojo Tulloh
Steve Tuffnell
Devin Tupper
Charlie Turnbull
Mike Turner
Neil Turner
Aisling Twomey
Eleanor Updegraff
Geoffrey Urland
Raminta Uselyte
Symon Vegro
Francesca Veneziano
Irene Verdiesen
Julia Wait
Susan Walby
Chris Walker
Craig Walker
Phoebe Walker
Stephen Walker
Ben Waller
Anna Walsh

Kevin Walsh
Sinead Walsh
Steve Walsh
Christopher Walthorne
Zhen Wang
Tahia Warda
Jerry Ward
Kate Ward
Peter Ward
Rachael Wardell
Guy Ware
Darren Waring
Diane Waring
Emma Warnock
Stephanie Wasek
Daniel Waterfield
Chris Watts
Sarah Webb
Ian Webster
Lucy Webster

Adam Welch
Joanna Wellings
Ian Wells
Karl Ruben Weseth
Jo West-Moore
Wendy Whidden
Robert White
Ben Wilder
Kyra Wilder
Gary Wilks
Claire Willerton
Andrea Willett
G Williams
Sharon Williams
Emma Wilson
Sarah Wiltshire
Kyle Winkler
Bianca Winter
Lucie Winter
Sheena Winter

Astrid Maria
  Wissenburg
Stephen Witkowski
Michael Wohl
Naomi Wood
Nathan Wood
Sarah Wood
Paul Woodgate
Emma Woolerton
Lorna Wright
Lydia Wynn
Lindsay Yates
Faye Young
Ian Young
Juliano Zaffino
Vanessa Zampiga
Sylvie Zannier
Rupert Ziziros
Carsten Zwaaneveld